U0080272
山田社

山田社

＼就是這麼簡單！／

情境模擬

旅遊英語

里昂 ◎著

1個句型 多個情境

MP3

「句型×單字」英語呱呱叫
用中學英語，照樣與全世界溝通

Where do you live? — I live in Taipei.
你住哪裡？ 我住在台北。

體驗更有趣、更不可思議！

山田社

一場疫情，讓世界變得不一樣。
宅在家，世界依然存在！
宅在家，一樣跟世界溝通！

宅在家，更要學英語，遠距溝通，線上直播等，讓您的才華、
商品可以進軍全世界。

疫情帶來了宅經濟的商機，遠距溝通、線上直播等成為熱門。利用遠距更快瞭解不同專業領域的人的思維，更能跳脫框架，理解與別人思維的差異。這時候想跟上世界腳步，更要學英語。

跟世界溝通，中學英語就很夠啦！萬丈高樓平地起，學英語會話，先從日常生活、情境模擬旅遊英語開始吧！

用中學英語，讓您不出國英語一樣呱呱叫！
用中學英語，就讓老外驚豔！
用中學英語，照樣與全世界溝通！

書中精選的中學英語句型與單字，讓您出國趴趴走、線上交老外朋友，走跳全世界都夠用。書中有日常問候、說說自己、聊天談興趣、也有交通、住宿、點餐、搭機、入境等豐富情境模擬主題。單字、文法不死背，單字套句型，天天自由選！可說是最佳的語言護照！

■ 要說，就要馬上可以說

書中告訴您，學英語不用想太多，只要巧妙使用套用術，也就是單字套用常用句的，一句句道地英語，便能輕鬆脫口而出，隨手寫。

■ 簡單4個步驟，說英語超有自信！

書中告訴您，打造出自信十足的英語，只要4個步驟—

Step1 87個聊天、旅遊必遇情境模擬場景。
Step2 老外24HR都在用的句型。
Step3 麻吉英單來作陣，套在句子真好用。
Step4 聽CD，練就最道地，最漂亮的老外腔。

本書內容安排最貼心，絕對是您旅遊的最佳幫手。紮紮實實的一小本，輕輕鬆鬆開口說英語、隨手寫，用英語就是快樂！

MP3-2

MP3-2

MP3-2

Part 1

日常簡單用語

日常用語

1 你好

你好！
Hello.

嗨！
Hi.

早安。
Good morning.

午安。
Good afternoon.

您好嗎？（初次見面 ）
How do you do?

你好嗎？
How are you?

很高興認識你！
Nice to meet you!

最近如何？
How's it going?

發生了什麼事？
What's up?

真高興(再)見到你。
Good to see you (again).

小小專欄

☆[Hi!]
是“招呼”的用語，但一般用在同年齡或比較親近的人。

2 再見

再見！
Good-bye.

再見！
Bye Bye.

回頭見。
See you later.

待回見。
Later.

晚安！
Good night.

祝你有美好的一天。
Have a nice day.

一路順風。
Have a good flight.

保重。
Take care.

放輕鬆一點。
Take it easy.

下次再見囉！
See you next time.

等會見！
See you around.

3 回答

是的。
Yes./Yeah.

是的，沒錯。
Yeah, right.

我明白。
I see./I think so.

原來如此。
Oh, that's why.

不，謝謝你。
No, thank you.

我不這麼認為。
I don't think so.

沒關係。
That's ok.

好 / 沒問題。
OK.

當然。
Sure.

可能吧。
Maybe.

真的嗎？
Really?

謝謝

非常感謝。

Thank you very much.

謝謝。

Thanks.

哇，你真好。

Wow, that's so nice of you.

謝謝你的幫忙。

Thanks for your help.

謝謝你抽空。

Thanks for your time.

萬分感謝。

Thanks a million.

真的很謝謝你。

Thanks a lot.

謝謝.我欠你一個人情。

Thanks. I owe you one.

謝謝.這是我的榮幸。

Thanks. I'd love to.

5 不客氣

不客氣。
You're welcome.

不必擔心這個。
Well, don't worry about it.

不客氣。
Not at all.

沒問題。
No problem.

這是我的榮幸。
My pleasure.

喔！那沒什麼。
Oh, it's nothing.

真的！那沒什麼。
Really, it's nothing much.

不要在意！
Don't mention it.

別擔心。
No worries.

要不然朋友是做什麼用的？(別跟我客氣)
What are friends for?

6 對不起

我很抱歉。

I'm sorry.

對不起。

Sorry.

我道歉。

I apologize.

我對那事感到遺憾。

I'm sorry about that.

噢…對不起。

Oops. Sorry.

請原諒我。

Please forgive me.

小小專欄

☆**[Oops!]**

表示驚訝、狼狽、謝罪等的叫聲。是相當於“啊、喔、唉”的感嘆詞。

7 借問一下

對不起。

Excuse me.

對不起，先生／小姐。

Excuse me, sir/ma'am.

請你告訴我…好嗎？

Would you please tell me...?

有誰知道…的嗎？

Does anybody know...?

對不起，能打擾你一分鐘嗎？

Excuse me, do you have a minute?

很抱歉打擾你，不過…。

Sorry to bother you, but...

我可以問／請求…。

May I ask...

8 請再說一次

請再說一次嗎？

Pardon?

請再說一次嗎？

Excuse me?

可以請你重複一遍嗎？

Could you please repeat that?

你介意再說一遍嗎？

Do you mind saying that again?

對不起,我剛剛沒有注意到。

I'm sorry, I didn't catch that.

你剛剛說什麼?

What did you say?

9 感歎詞

（表示驚奇等）啊！糟了！

Gosh!

（表示驚訝、讚賞等）哇！咦！啊！

Gee!

這個嘛！

Well!

真是的！

Shoot!

哎喲！

Oops!

得了吧！

Come on!

噢，天啊！

Oh, my!

沒這回事！

No way!

酷！

Cool!

太棒了！

Great!

我的旅遊小筆記

旅遊英語

Part 2

基本數字

1 數字

A **How many?**

多少？

B —**Six.**

—6。

1	2	3	4
one	**two**	**three**	**four**
5	6	7	8
five	**six**	**seven**	**eight**
9	10	11	12
nine	**ten**	**eleven**	**twelve**
13	14	15	16
thirteen	**fourteen**	**fifteen**	**sixteen**
17	18	19	20
seventeen	**eighteen**	**nineteen**	**twenty**
21	22	23	24
twenty-one	**twenty-two**	**twenty-three**	**twenty-four**

25	26	27	28
twenty-five	twenty-six	twenty-seven	twenty-eight
29	30	31	32
twenty-nine	thirty	thirty-one	thirty-two
33	34	35	36
thirty-three	thirty-four	thirty-five	thirty-six
37	38	39	40
thirty-seven	thirty-eight	thirty-nine	forty
41	42	43	44
forty-one	forty-two	forty-three	forty-four
45	46	47	48
forty-five	forty-six	forty-seven	forty-eight
49	50	51	52
forty-nine	fifty	fifty-one	fifty-two
53	54	55	56
fifty-three	fifty-four	fifty-five	fifty-six

57
fifty-seven

58
fifty-eight

59
fifty-nine

60
sixty

70
seventy

80
eighty

90
ninety

100
one hundred

110
one hundred and ten

120
one hundred and twenty

130
one hundred and thirty

140
one hundred and forty

150
one hundred and fifty

160
one hundred and sixty

170
one hundred and seventy

180
one hundred and eighty

190
one hundred and ninety

200
two hundred

300
three hundred

400
four hundred

500
five hundred

600
six hundred

700
seven hundred

800
eight hundred

900
nine hundred

1000
one thousand

1001
one thousand and one

2000
two thousand

3000
three thousand

4000
four thousand

5000
five thousand

6000
six thousand

7000
seven thousand

8000
eight thousand

9000
nine thousand

一萬
ten thousand

十萬
one hundred thousand

一 萬
one million

一千萬
ten million

一億
one hundred million

十億
one billion

2 星期

今週の予定 WEEKLY
	mon 月	
／	tue 火	
／	wed 水	
／	thu 木	
／	fri 金	
／	sat 土	

A When is your test?
你什麼時候考試？

B —This Friday.
—這星期五。

星期天
Sunday

星期一
Monday

星期二
Tuesday

星期三
Wednesday

星期四
Thursday

星期五
Friday

星期六
Saturday

3 時間

A What time is it now?
現在幾點了？

B —It's six o'clock.
—現在六點。

一點鐘
one o'clock

兩點鐘
two o'clock

三點鐘
three o'clock

四點鐘
four o'clock

五點鐘
five o'clock

六點鐘
six o'clock

七點鐘

seven o'clock

八點鐘

eight o'clock

九點鐘

nine o'clock

十點鐘

ten o'clock

十一點鐘

eleven o'clock

十二點鐘

twelve o'clock

6點

six(o'clock)

6點10分

six ten

6點15分

six fifteen

6點24分

six twenty-four

6點30分

six thirty

6點54分

six fifty-four

小小專欄

☆**[hour, o'clock]** 這兩字有什麼不同，**“o'clock”**是**“of the clock”**的縮寫，表示幾點鐘之意。而**“hour”**是指一個小時的時間。

好用單字

10分鐘
10 minutes

15分鐘
15 minutes

30分鐘
30 minutes

1個小時
an(1)hour

2個小時
2 hours

2個半小時
2 and a half hours

一天
one day

半天
half a day

再5分四點
5 minutes before four o'clock

再10分八點
10 to 8

30分内
in 30 minutes

1小時内
in an hour

2、3分内
in a few minutes

午前，上午
a.m.

午後，下午
p.m.

4 月份

A **What's the date today?**

今天是幾月幾號？

B **—It's May 5th.**

—今天是五月五號。

一月	二月	三月	四月
January	**February**	**March**	**April**
五月	**六月**	**七月**	**八月**
May	**June**	**July**	**August**
九月	**十月**	**十一月**	**十二月**
September	**October**	**November**	**December**

5 日期

A **When is your birthday?**

你什麼時候生日?

B **—It's August 21st.**

—是八月二十一日。

一日	二日
the first 1st	the second 2nd
三日	四日
the third 3rd	the fourth 4th
五日	六日
the fifth 5th	sixth 6th
七日	十一日
seventh 7th	eleventh 11th
十二日	二十二日
twelfth 12th	22nd
二十三日	三十一日
23rd	31st

小小專欄

☆從「6日」到「19日」除了“**twelve**”要去字尾“**ve**”加“**fth**”及“**nine**”要去“**e**”加“**th**”外，其餘在數字後面加上“**th**”就是日期了。

我的旅遊小筆記

Part 3

跟自己有關的話題

一、說說自己

1 我的名字

A **What's your name?**

你叫什麼名字？

B **—My name is <u>Meg Ryan</u>**

—我叫<u>梅格萊恩</u>。

陳美玲
Meiling Chen

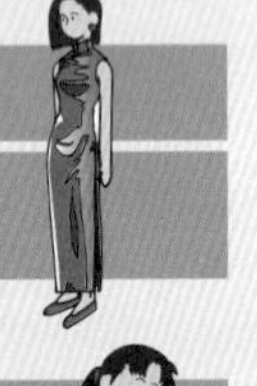

金博撒冷
Kimber Salen

鈴木山崎
Suzuki Yamazaki

大衛舒茲
David Shultz

吳明
Ming Wu

芮妮布迪厄
Renee Boudrieu

2 我姓史密斯

A What's your last name?

你姓什麼？

B —Smith.

—史密斯。

詹森 Johnson	威廉 William
瓊斯 Jones	布朗 Brown
大衛 David	米勒 Miller
威爾遜 Wilson	莫爾 Moore
泰勒 Taylor	安德森 Anderson
湯瑪士 Thomas	傑克遜 Jackson

懷特	White
哈利	Harley
馬丁	Martin
湯馬士	Thompson
賈西亞	Garcia
馬丁尼茲	Martinez
羅賓森	Robinson

例句

你好，我是泰利。

Hello, I'm Terry.

我的名字是美玲，姓陳。

My first name is Meiling and my family name is Chen.

您好。

How do you do?

很高興認識你。

Nice to meet you.

很高興認識你。

Glad to meet you.

很高興認識您。

Pleased to meet you.

很榮幸認識您。

It's a pleasure to meet you.

你叫什麼名字？

What's your name?

你今天過的如何？

How are you today?

一切都還好吧？

How is everything?

小小專欄

☆跟初次見面的人，一般用[How do you do?]來問候對方，這時候對方要重複這一句話來回敬問候，而且一般不做具體的回答。也就是，

How do you do?

— How do you do?

☆相對地，跟自己熟悉的人見面時，一般用[How are you?]，這時候對方通常要作出回答。例如，

How are you?

— Fine,thank you.

☆[Nice to meet you.]也是第一次見面寒暄致意用的，說法比[How do you do?]親切、隨和。第一次見面，跟對方寒暄致意以後，接下來的話題一般是詢問對方的工作或是學習（旅行）情況。

3 我來自台灣

A **Where are you from?**

你從哪裡來？

B **—I'm from <u>Taiwan</u>.**

—我來自台灣。

中國
China

美國
the U.S.A

日本
Japan

加拿大
Canada

韓國
Korea

北韓
North Korea

印度
India

新加坡
Singapore

馬來西亞
Malaysia

菲律賓
the Philippines

泰國
Thailand

俄羅斯
Russia

瑞典
Sweden

瑞士
Switzerland

英國
England

法國
France

西班牙
Spain

義大利
Italy

德國
Germany

荷蘭
the Netherlands

希臘
Greece

古巴
Cuba

墨西哥
Mexico

阿根
Argentina

智利
Chile

巴西
Brazil

秘魯

Peru

澳大利亞

Australia

紐西蘭

New Zealand

埃及

Egypt

肯亞

Kenya

小小專欄

☆我們看到老外，常喜歡問[**Where are you from?**]或者是[**Where do you come from?**]，意思是“你來自哪裡?”這可是具有“你在哪裡出生?”跟“你在哪裡成長?”兩重意義的喔！所以回答的時候，可以根據當時的會話內容，選擇回答的方式。

☆在被問到故鄉時，美國人習慣以居住時間最久的地方來回答。例如，

Where are you from?

— **I was born in Los Angeles, but I grew up in Boston.**

Where do you come from?

— **I come from Taipei.**

4 我住在台北

A Where do you live?

你住哪裡？

B —I live in Taipei.

—我住在台北。

北（中國）
Beijing(China)

華盛頓(美國)
Washington(U.S.A)

東（日本）
Tokyo(Japan)

首爾(南韓)
Seoul(Korea)

平壤(北韓)
Pyongyang(North Korea)

新德里(印度)
New Delhi(India)

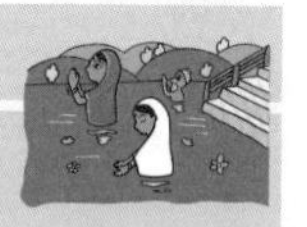

新加坡(新加坡)
Singapore(Singapore)

吉隆坡(馬來西亞)
Kuala Lumpur(Malaysia)

馬尼拉(菲律賓)
Manila(Philippines)

曼谷(泰國)
Bangkok(Thailand)

羅馬(義大利)
Rome(Italy)

倫敦(英國)
London(England)

巴黎(法國)
Paris(France)

馬德里(西班牙)
Madrid(Spain)

伯恩(瑞士)
Bern(Switzerland)

柏林(德國)
Berlin(Germany)

莫斯科(俄羅斯)
Moscow(Russia)

斯德哥爾摩(瑞典)
Stockholm(Sweden)

布宜諾賽利斯(阿根)
Buenos Aires(Argentina)

聖地牙哥(智利)
Santiago(Chile)

阿姆斯特丹(荷蘭)
Amsterdam(Netherlands)

雅典(希臘)
Athens(Greece)

哈瓦那(古巴)
Havana(Cuba)

墨西哥城(墨西哥)
Mexico city(Mexico)

巴西利亞(巴西)
Brasilia(Brazil)

利馬(祕魯)
Lima(Peru)

坎培拉(澳洲)
Canberra(Australia)

威靈頓(紐西蘭)
Wellington(New Zealand)

開羅(埃及)
Cairo(Egypt)

奈洛比(肯亞)
Nairobi(Kenya)

例句

我是台灣人。
I'm Taiwanese.

你是來自美國的嗎?
Are you from the USA?

我住在洛杉磯。
I live in Los Angeles.

你英文說的真好。
You speak English very well.

我會說一點點英文。
I speak a little English.

你學英文有多久了?
How long have you studied English?

學了好幾個月。
For several months.

你會說中文嗎?
Can you speak Chinese?

我會說一點點(這種語言)。

I can speak a little bit.

這是你第一次來這裡參觀／出國旅遊嗎？

Is this your first time visiting here / traveling overseas?

你在哪裡長大？

Where did you grow up?

很高興認識你。

Nice to meet you.

小小專欄

☆如果對方只是應酬式的稱讚你英文很好，請不要慌張地說：“**no**”。請這樣說：［**Thank you, but I only speak a little.**］。這樣回答就很恰當了。

5 我是英文老師

A **What do you do?**

你從事什麼工作?

B —**I'm an English teacher.**

—我是英文老師。

醫生

a doctor

護士

a nurse

律師

a lawyer

商人

a businessperson

作家

a writer

電腦程式員

a computer programmer

記者

a reporter

學生

a student

服裝設計師

a fashion designer

警察

police officer

例句

我在貿易公司工作。

I work in a trading company.

我為政府工作。

I work for the government.

我有自己的事業。

I run my own business.

我開了一家理髮店。

I have a barbershop.

我在大學教書。
I teach in a university.

我是全職的家庭主婦。
I'm a full-time housewife.

我是家庭主婦。
I'm a homemaker.

我是自己經營做生意。
I'm self-employed.

我退休了。
I'm retired.

我是兼職的保姆。
I'm a part-time baby sitter.

好用單字

全職
full-time

兼職
part-time

待業中
unemployed

正在找工作 / 待職中
looking for a job

剛畢業
just graduated from school

剛退伍
just got out of the army

6 我想當棒球選手

A What do you want to be?

你想要從事什麼工作?

B —A baseball player.

—棒球選手

作家

A writer

翻譯員

A translator

電視節目製作人

A TV producer

導遊

A tour guide

老師

A teacher

歌手

A singer

科學家

A scientist

總統

A president

企劃者

A planner

護士

A nurse

音樂家
A musician

模特兒
A model

流行設計師
A fashion designer

編輯
An editor

舞蹈家
A dancer

外交官
A diplomat

牙醫
A dentist

電影明星
A movie star

律師
A lawyer

工程師
An engineer

醫生
A doctor

程式設計員
A computer programmer

主播
An anchor

這是楊先生

A **This is Mr. Yang.**

這位是楊先生。

B —**Nice to meet you.**

—很高興見到你。

王	陳
Wang	**Chen**
林	黃
Lin	**Huang**
張	李
Chang	**Li**
吳	劉
Wu	**Liu**
蔡	
Cai	

二、介紹家人

1 這是我爸爸

This is my father.

這是我爸爸。

媽媽
mother

哥哥
older brother

弟弟
younger brother

姊姊
older sister

妹妹
younger sister

妻子
wife

丈夫
husband

叔叔、舅舅
uncle

姨媽、姑姑
aunt

表兄弟姐妹
cousin

姪女、外甥女
niece

姪子、外甥
nephew

兒子
son

女兒
daughter

祖父

grandfather

祖母

grandmother

朋友

friend

摯友

best friend

老闆

boss

同事

co-worker

未婚夫

fiance

未婚妻

fiancee

女朋友

girlfriend

男朋友

boyfriend

前男友

former boyfriend

前女友

former girlfriend

例句

我有一個女兒。

I have a daughter.

他們是我的父母。

They are my parents.

我是家裡的獨生子（獨生女）。

I'm an only child.

我沒有兒女。

I don't have any kids.

我有一個弟弟和兩個妹妹。
I have a brother and two sisters.

我是家裡最小的孩子。
I'm the youngest in my family.

我媽媽很早就去世了。
My mom passed away.

我爸爸獨自撫養我們長大。
My dad raised us by himself.

他必須非常辛苦的工作。
He had to work very hard.

我們互相照顧對方。
We took care of each other.

他不會再婚。
He never remarried.

我們非常想念我們的母親。
We miss our mom very much.

小小專欄

☆若是姻親關係的名稱，則加上"**in-law**"。例如："**mother-in-law**"是婆婆或岳母，"**sister-in-law**"是妯娌或姨子。

2 哥哥是汽車行銷員

你哥哥從事什麼工作的?
What does your brother do?

我哥哥是汽車經銷商。
My brother is a car dealer.

他在一家速食餐廳打工。
He works part-time in a fast food restaurant.

我爸爸擁有一間婚紗攝影室。
My dad has a wedding studio.

她就讀研究所。
She's in graduate school.

她在都市銀行工作。
She works at City Bank.

他們是開花店的。
They are florists.

他剛退伍。
He just got out of the army.

他正在找工作。
He is between jobs.

我的哥哥／弟弟從事他技術專長的工作。
My brother is working on his skill set.

他正在找工作。
He is looking for a job.

他正在接受許多公司的面試。
He is interviewing at several firms.

小小專欄

☆在英文中打工的人叫"**part-time worker**"或"**a part-timer**"；而一天工作8小時的全職人員叫"**a full-time worker**"或"**a full-timer**"。

3 我妹妹有點害羞

My sister is a little shy.

我妹妹有一點害羞。

溫柔
gentle

安靜
quiet

外向
outgoing

固執
stubborn

勤快
diligent

慷慨
generous

急性子
hot-tempered

吝嗇的、小氣的
stingy

例句

我姐妹是個可愛的女生。
My sister is a sweet girl.

我兄弟沒有女朋友。
My brother doesn't have a girlfriend.

他擅長運動。
He is good at sports.

她網球打得很好。
She plays tennis very well.

她住在香港。
She lives in Hong Kong.

我父親非常隨和。
My father is very easygoing.

我的朋友都很喜愛我的父母親。
My friends love my parents.

我女兒主修音樂。
My daughter majors in music.

我姐妹很堅持己見。
My sister keeps to herself a lot.

她很聰明，不過她不太發表意見。
She's very smart, but she doesn't say much.

她喜歡畫畫,閱讀,和彈鋼琴。

She enjoys drawing, reading, and playing the piano.

她朋友不多,不過她很喜歡一個人獨處。

She has a few friends, but she enjoys spending time alone.

小小專欄

☆我們來比較：

[drawing , painting]

drawing:一般是指單純以鉛筆或筆素描的線條畫，或是描化設計而不上色的圖畫。

painting:指的是用帶有顏色的顏料（如水彩，油墨），繪製而成的畫。

好用單字

可愛的、小巧玲瓏的	cute
漂亮的、秀麗的	pretty
苗條的、纖細的	slim
胖嘟嘟的、豐滿的	chubby
肥胖的	fat
皮包骨的、極瘦的	skinny
已婚的、有配偶的	married
單身的、未婚的	single
離婚的	divorced
單身漢	bachelor

三、談天氣

1 今天真熱

It's hot today.

今天真熱。

涼快的
cool

冷的、寒冷的
cold

多雲的、陰天的
cloudy

溫暖的、暖和的
warm

潮濕的
humid

有霧的、多霧的
foggy

颼風的、多風的
windy

下雨的、多雨的
rainy

小小專欄

☆我們來比較：

[cool, cold, chilly, freezing]

cool：涼爽而令人感到舒適宜人的溫度。

cold：溫度低到令人感到寒冷不舒服的樣子。

chilly：比cold更冷，形容會讓人打寒顫的冰冷。

freezing：冷到已經讓人覺得要被凍僵的嚴寒。

例句

今天天氣如何？

How's the weather today?

天氣真棒。

The weather is great.

天氣晴朗。

It's a sunny day.

下著大雨。

It's raining hard.

多雲。

It's cloudy.

天氣看起來好像要下雨。

It looks like it's going to rain.

我們這裡明天颱颱風。

We'll have a typhoon tomorrow.

天啊！天氣變得那麼快。

Man! It changed so fast.

外面風還蠻大的。

It's pretty windy out there.

真是個萬里晴空的日子！

What a clear day!

氣溫幾度？

What's the temperature?

34度。

It's 34 degrees.

今天天氣熱的要沸騰了。

It's boiling.

今天冷的要結冰了。

It's freezing.

今天的天氣很適合做戶外活 。

It's quite pleasant outside today.

今天有微微的起風。

There's a light / gentle breeze.

今天天色有些陰暗。

It's a little overcast.

今天是適合出去走走的好日子。

It's a great day to go outside.

小小專欄

☆在詢問天氣的時候，一般習慣說[What's the weather?]，也有直接問「氣溫幾度」，這時候就說[What's the temperature?]，而回答就說[It's…degress.]。

☆[How's the weather today?]的"How's"是"How is"的縮寫。

☆在美國，日常生活所使用的溫度單位是"fahrenheit"。攝氏零度等於華氏的三十二度。

好用單字

度、度數（℃）

degree(s)

攝氏溫度

Centigrade

華氏溫度

Fahrenheit

溫度計

thermometer

2 紐約天氣怎麼樣

How is the weather in New York?
紐約的天氣怎麼樣?

春天
spring

夏天
summer

秋天
fall/autumn

冬天
winter

小小專欄

☆ "**weather**"（天氣）通常是指今天或是短時間之內、經常改變的天氣狀態。另外，"**climate**"（氣候）指某個地方長期的天氣狀態，包括雨量、風向、平均溫度等。

例句

夏天炎熱。
It's hot in the summer.

有時候下午會下雨。
It rains sometimes in the afternoon.

在這裡，秋天是最棒的季節。

Fall is the best season of the year here.

這裡天氣涼快的程度和加州差不多。

The weather is about as cool as it is in California.

雨季是從四月到八月。

The rainy season is from April to August.

一月份和二月份常常會下雪。

It snows often in January and February.

春天是很美妙的。

Spring is lovely.

這裡的冬天通常很寒冷。

The winters are usually chilly here.

在夏天，我很喜歡去中央公園聽免費的音樂演奏會。

During the summer, I love to go to Central Park and listen to the free concerts.

小小專欄

☆我們來比較：

「**in, at, on**」

in：空間上指某個比較大的場所，如國家、城市，表示在 之內。時間上指在某一段比較長的時段(年、月)中。如“**in the summer**”（在夏天）。

at：空間上指某個較小的特定地點，如車站、村落。時間上也是指比較小、精確的時間，如幾點“**at seven o'clock**”（在7點）。

on：對於空間上指與某物接觸或是靠近的上方。時間上指在某個特定的日子中，如“**on Sunday**”（在星期天）。

3 明天會下雨嗎

Will we have rain tomorrow?

明天會下雨嗎？

雪	雨
snow	rain

颱風	雷陣雨
a typhoon	thundershowers

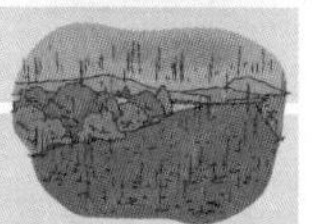

霧	颶風
fog	a hurricane

冰雹	冷鋒面
hail	a cold front

例句

本週末會變得比較涼快。

It will become cooler this weekend.

本週三會刮颱風。

We'll have a typhoon this Wednesday.

明天的天氣如何？

How will the weather be tomorrow?

明天可能會下雨。

It might rain tomorrow.

傍晚溫度會下降2至3度。

The temperature will drop 2 to 3 degrees in the evening.

明天會是風和日麗的好天氣。

It's going to be nice and sunny tomorrow.

小小專欄

☆[The temperature will drop 2 to 3 degrees in the evening.]中的“drop”指突然下降，或是數量、強度、容量等單位的減少，或是像是水滴般一點一點落下的。含有迅速往正下方落下的意思。

四、談個

我的生日是三月二十四日

A When is your birthday?

你的生日在什麼時候?

B —My birthday is on <u>March 24th</u>.

—我的生日是<u>三月二十四日</u>。

一月二十日
January twentieth
JANUARY

二月二日
February second
FEBRUARY

三月十六日
March sixteenth
MARCH

四月一日
April first
APRIL

五月十四日
May fourteenth
MAY

六月十一日
June eleventh
JUNE

七月三日
July third
JULY

八月八日
August eighth
AUGUST

九月二十三日
September twenty-third
SEPTEMBER

十月十七日
October seventh
OCTOBER

十一月十日

November tenth

十二月五日

December fifth

例句

你是幾年出生的？

What year were you born?

我是1975年出生的。

I was born in 1975.

我的生日是在五月。

My birthday is in May.

你會在生日做些什麼？

What will you do on your birthday?

我今年就二十歲了。

I will be twenty this year.

明天你會來參加我的生日宴會嗎?

Will you come to my birthday party tomorrow?

小小專欄

☆除非是很熟的朋友，否則問人幾年出生的有點沒禮貌哦！

生日的日期是用序數，例如一號為**first**，二號為**second.**

☆1975年讀成**nineteen seventy-five**.

2 我是雙子座

A What's your sign?

你是什麼星座呢?

B —I'm a Gemini.

—我是雙子座。

白羊座
an Aries

金牛座
a Taurus

雙子座
a Gemini

巨蟹座
a Cancer

獅子座
a Leo

處女座
a Virgo

天秤座
a Libra

天蠍座
a Scorpio

射手座
a Sagittarius

摩羯座
a Capricorn

水瓶座

an Aquarius

雙魚座

a Pisces

例句

我猜你是處女座。

I bet you are a Virgo.

雙魚座非常有藝術氣息。

Pisces are very artistic.

射手座很活潑外向。

Sagittarius are active and out-going.

你完全不像天秤座。

You are not like a Libra at all.

我不相信那套玩意兒。

I don't believe in that kind of stuff.

這完全不合理。

It just doesn't make any sense.

你每天都會看你的星座運勢嗎？

Do you read your horoscope every day?

我媽媽和我太太都是魔羯座的。

My mother is a Capricorn and so is my wife.

我認為星座占卜很有意思。

I think astrology is very interesting.

巨蟹座是很情緒化的。

Cancers are highly emotional.

小小專欄

☆[I think astrology is very interesting.]中的“interesting”形容因為有知識性的趣味，而讓人產生好奇和興趣的。

好用單字

雅緻的、優美的	**elegant**
吹毛求疵的、挑剔的	**picky**
獨立的、自主的	**independent**
樂觀的	**optimistic**
有耐性的、能忍受的	**patient**
隨和的	**easygoing**
倔強的、頑固的	**stubborn**
悲觀的	**pessimistic**
妒忌的	**jealous**
沒耐性的	**impatient**

3 我覺得她很多愁善感

I think she's very sentimental.

我覺得她很多愁善感。

浪漫的、多情的	被動的、消極的
romantic	**passive**
主動的、活潑的	負責任的、可信賴的
active	**responsible**
敏感的、靈敏的	擅長交際的
sensitive	**sociable**
思想狹隘的	忠誠的
narrow-minded	**loyal**

例句

我受不了她！

I can't stand her!

她就是不能閉嘴。

She never shuts up.

我想她只是遇到困境。

I think she's just having a hard time.

我對某些事情抱持極端負面的想法。

I'm very negative about some things.

你常常以正面的想法看事情。

You always look on the bright side.

你真是非常仁慈。

You really are very kind.

他正好不是我喜歡的那一型。

He's just not my type.

他經常道人長短。

He gossips a lot.

她使我感到緊張。

She gets on my nerves.

我對他沒什麼興趣。

I'm not too keen on him.

我覺得我們很合得來。

I think we're pretty compatible.

我們相處愉快。

We get along great.

我倆是天生的一對。

We are perfect for one another.

我迷戀上她了。

I have a crush on her.

他百分百的真誠。

He is totally sincere.

五、興趣與嗜好

我喜歡看小說

A **What do you like to do on the weekend?**
你週末喜歡做什麼?

B **—I love reading novels.**
—我喜歡閱讀小說。

逛街
to go shopping

看電視
watching TV

遠足
to go hiking

和家人共度
spending time with my family

和朋友去KTV唱歌
going to KTV with friends

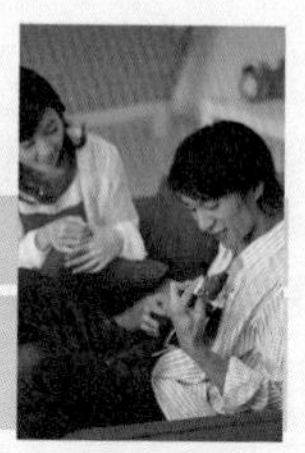

只要跟你在一起

just being with you

看電影

going to the movies

小小專欄

☆**[watching TV]**中的“**watch**”表示集中注意力，專心的觀看某個正在動作的物體（如運動、事態的變化）。比“**look**”（看）看的時間要長。

例句

我喜歡開車兜風。

I like driving around.

我喜歡旅行。

I like to go traveling.

我什麼都不能做，因為我要工作。

I can't do anything, I have to work.

不做什麼。只在家裡休息。

Nothing special. Just resting at home.

我週末有兼差的工作。

I have a part-time job on the weekend.

我喜歡去看棒球比賽。

I like to go to a baseball game.

明天我們要外出去旅行。

Tomorrow we will go out for a trip.

我一直都很期待這次旅行。

I'm really looking forward to this.

這聽起來很有趣。

That sounds fun.

這非常恐怖。

That's awful.

我是個注重家庭的人。

I'm more of a homebody myself.

我喜歡從事戶外活 。

I love doing things outdoors.

他最愛的休閒娛樂是做填字遊戲。

Her favorite pastime is doing crossword puzzles.

他和他的鄰居打麻將。

He plays mahjong with his neighbors.

我喜歡和我的朋友一起去喝點小酒。

I like to get together with my friends for a drink.

我週末喜歡去拜訪朋友。

I like to visit friends on the weekend.

小小專欄

☆美國人很喜歡利用週末假日到戶外活動。其中“**fishing trips**”（釣魚）是美國最普遍的休閒活動之一。但要注意的是，隨便垂釣可能是違法的，在很多州裡，釣魚可是要買釣魚執照的喔！垂釣前最好查好各州在這方面的規定喔！

☆我們常聽到的“**habit**”（嗜好）是指個人因為長久養成的某些無意識的習慣或是動作。

2 我喜歡打籃球

A **Do you like sports?**

你喜歡運動嗎?

B **—Yeah, I love playing basketball.**

—喜歡，我喜歡打籃球。

美式足球

football

足球

soccer

高爾夫球

golf

網球

tennis

羽毛球

badminton

曲棍球

hockey

排球

volleyball

壘球

softball

乒乓球

ping-pong

壁球、迴力球

squash

例句

我是洋基隊的忠實球迷。

I'm a big Yankees fan.

我不會錯過ESPN播放的任何一場比賽。

I never miss a game on ESPN.

我喜歡看美式足球賽。

I love football games.

你想要找個時間一起打網球嗎？

Do you want to play tennis together sometime?

好的，我們找個時間打球吧。

Yeah, let's do it sometime.

這個嘛，我不太擅長運動。

Well, I'm not too good at sports.

籃球是我喜愛的運動。

Basketball is my favorite sport.

你知道怎麼滑水嗎？

Do you know how to water-ski?

我是第一次滑水。

This is my first time.

你會跳水嗎？

Can you dive?

我很喜歡跳水。

I like diving very much.

不，我不知道。

No, I don't know how.

我在高中時打棒球。

I played baseball in high school.

我喜歡游泳勝於慢跑。

I prefer swimming to jogging.

他真是一個網球選手。

He is quite a tennis player.

明天要不要去衝浪?

Would you like to go surfing tomorrow?

我寧願爬過碎玻璃也不會支持紐約洋基隊。(我怎麼樣也不會支持紐約洋基隊)

I'd rather crawl over broken glass than root for the New York Yankees。 (Joke =P)

小小專欄

☆**[Do you know how to water ski?]**裡的"**water-ski**"是動詞，不是名詞！它的意思是「去做滑水的動作」。"**water-skiing**"才是名詞，意思是「滑水運動」。「**How to+** 詞＋名詞」表示「知道怎麼去 …」的意思。

☆**[Do you know how to dive?]**是問對方是否知道進行的方法。而**[Can you dive?]**是問對方會不會做。

3 我不玩團隊運動，但我游泳

I don't do team sports, but I swim.

我不玩團隊運動，但我游泳。

騎腳踏車
go biking / cycling

釣魚
go fishing

做有氧運動
do aerobics

慢跑
go jogging

空手道
do karate

衝浪
go surfing

做瑜珈
do yoga

攀岩
go rock climbing

滑雪
go skiing

去健身房健身
work out in the gym

例句

你做運動嗎？

Do you do exercises?

你多久去一次健身房健身？

How often do you work out in the gym?

哇！ 這聽起來很有趣。

Wow, that sounds fun.

這很難嗎？

Is that difficult?

我不看ESPN的。

I don't watch ESPN.

你喜歡登山旅行嗎？

Did you enjoy the mountaineering trip?

我很喜歡。

I liked it very much.

我喜歡自己一個人運動。

I enjoy exercising on my own.

我會督促自己直到我的極限。

I like to push myself as hard as I can.

她跑過馬拉松。

She has run a marathon.

他一個禮拜做三次體能訓練。

He works out three times a week.

要去潛水的裝備妳都帶齊了嗎?

Do you have everything you need to go snorkeling?

我的嗜好是收集卡片

A **What's your hobby?**

你的嗜好是什麼?

B **-My hobby is collecting cards.**

–我的嗜好是收集卡片。

聽音樂

listening to music

唱卡拉OK

karaoke

看電影

watching movies

閱讀

reading

看電視

watching TV

上網

browsing the Internet

玩電視遊樂器

playing video games

畫圖

drawing pictures

彈鋼琴

playing the piano

彈吉他

playing the guitar

烹飪
cooking

旅遊
traveling

騎自行車
cycling

開車兜風
going for a drive

攝影
taking photos

溜冰
skiing

游泳
swimming

購物
shopping

高爾夫
golf

和朋友聊天
chatting with friends

泡溫泉
going to hot spring resorts

網球
tennis

慢跑
jogging

看棒球比賽
watching baseball

看籃球比賽
watching basketball games

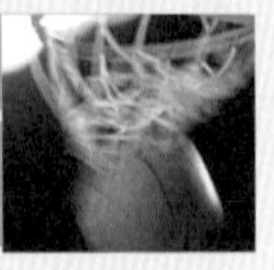

下棋
playing chess

寫書法
penmanship / calligraphy

縫紉
sewing

小小專欄

☆hobby / pastime

[What's your hobby?]中的"hobby"（嗜好）指業餘的休閒嗜好、興趣。因為個人的興趣而收集、做什麼東西；還有一個源自法語"pastime"（休閒活 ），是指閒暇時間所做的休閒活動，如閱讀、聽音樂、觀看棒球比賽等。

我喜歡動作片

六、談電影、電視與音樂

A What kind of movies do you like?

你喜歡什麼類型的電影？

B —I like action movies.

—我喜歡動作片。

愛情片	戲劇
romance movies	dramas
悲劇	喜劇
tragedies	comics
動畫	懸疑片
animations	mysteries
科幻片	恐怖片
science-fiction/sci-fi	horror movies

例句

「親家路窄」是我喜愛的喜劇。

***Meet the Parents* is my favorite comedy.**

天吶！這是一部很傷感的電影。

Man! That was a sad movie.

喔，這是一部經典電影。

Oh, that's a classic.

很有趣，而且很刺激。

It was very interesting and exciting.

我真的太喜歡這個角色了！

I really love that character.

和電影相比，我更喜歡座談性節目。

I prefer talk shows to movies.

音效做得真棒！

The sound effects are great.

是的，卡司陣容堅強。

Yeah, just a big cast.

最後一幕叫人非常沮喪。

The last scene is very depressing.

男主角的演技太棒了！

The hero's acting is wonderful.

我也是。

Me too!

我一個月大概會看一兩次電影。

I go to the movies once or twice a month.

我喜歡獨立製作的電影，但是我女朋友喜歡好萊塢式的大卡司電影。

I enjoy independent films, but my girlfriend prefers Hollywood blockbusters.

這部電影獲得了六項奧斯卡獎。

That movie won six Academy Awards/Oscars.

我父母喜歡看老式電影。

My parents love old movies.

小小專欄

☆**[Shall we watch TV?]**中的“**Shall we...**”用在提出建議，徵求對方意見的時候，相當於中文的“我們…好嗎？”

☆**[look at , watch, see]**都是“看”的意思，但使用上有些不同。“**look at**”強調有意識的去看的動作。“**watch**”表示集中注意力，專心的觀看某個正在動作的物體（如運動、事態的變化）。比“**look**”看的時間長。“**see**”指眼睛自然地看到。強調看到的結果。

☆**[Me too!]**常用來表示跟對方具有相同的看法、感受、觀點及要求等。

好用單字

票房賣座	劇情
box-office hit	**plot**

預告片	最佳電影
preview	best picture

男主角	女配角
leading actor	supporting actress

視覺效果	主題
visual effects	theme

2 你喜歡古典樂嗎?

Do you like classical music?

你喜歡古典樂嗎?

古典音樂	流行樂
classical music	popular music

爵士樂
jazz

歌劇
opera

重金屬
heavy metal

搖滾樂
rock and roll

情歌
love songs

鄉村音樂
country music

抒情音樂
soft music

饒舌
rap

藍調音樂
R&B rhythm & blues

交響樂
symphony

例句

我喜歡它的歌詞。
I like the lyrics.

我不喜歡重音樂。
I don't like the strong beat.

我想去聽音樂會。

I want to go to the concert.

音樂會如何？

How was the concert?

他有很棒的嗓子。

He has a great voice.

這個嘛，我受不了饒舌。

Well, I can't stand rap.

古典音樂常讓我想睡覺。

Classical music puts me to sleep.

比莉哈樂黛是我喜愛的爵士歌手。

Billie Holiday is my favorite jazz singer.

我是看心情選擇我聽的音樂。

What music I listen to depends on my mood.

大部分的年輕人喜歡嘻哈音樂。

Most young people like hip-hop.

我想去買那張CD。

I want to get that CD.

小小專欄

☆[How was the concert?]中的“How”表示「怎麼樣」，用來詢問對方的意見或感想時，常用過去式。例如，

How was your trip? （旅遊愉快嗎？）

How was the test? （考試考得怎麼樣？）

How was school today? （今天學校情況怎麼樣？）

Part 4

旅遊會話

一、在飛機上

我要柳丁汁

A **Would you like something to drink?**

你想要喝點飲料嗎？

B —**<u>Orange juice</u>, please.**

—<u>橘子汁</u>，謝謝。

咖啡

Coffee

茶

Tea

蘋果汁

Apple juice

汽水

Soda

水

Water

紅酒

Red wine

啤酒

Beer

奶昔

A milk shake

例句

不要加冰塊，謝謝你。

No ice, please.

再來一杯啤酒，謝謝你。

Another beer, please.

來些花生，謝謝你。

Some peanuts, please.

吸管，謝謝你。

A straw, please.

多加一點冰塊，謝謝你。

More ice, please.

再回沖一些咖啡，謝謝你。

A refill, please.

請給我一整罐。

The whole can, please.

雞尾酒要多少錢？

How much is a cocktail？

這是現搾的新鮮果汁嗎？

Is the juice fresh-squeezed？

麻煩一下，我要去咖啡因的。

Decaf, please.

你們有供應綠茶嗎？

Do you have green tea？

請給我一杯黑咖啡。

A black coffee, please.

2 給我雞肉飯

A Chicken rice or fish noodles？

要雞肉飯還是魚排麵？

B —<u>Chicken</u>, please.

—<u>雞肉</u>，謝謝你。

麵包
Bread

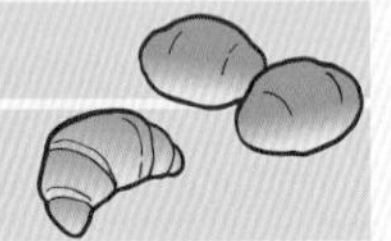

沙拉
Salad

水果
Fruit

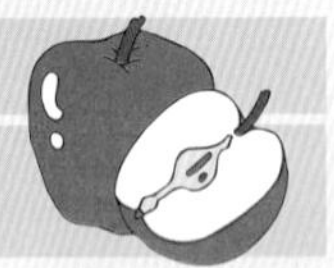

牛肉
Beef

豬肉
Pork

素菜餐
Avegetarian meal

兒童餐
A child's meal

牛排
Steak

例句

我已經叫了一份嬰兒餐。
I ordered an infant meal.

你們有沒有泡麵？
Do you have instant noodles？

我可以再要一份餐嗎？

Can I have another meal？

可以，如果我們有剩的話。

Yes, if we have any left.

對不起，我們只剩魚麵。

Sorry, we only have fish noodles left.

可以請你幫我清一下餐盤嗎？

Can you please clear my tray？

幾點開始供應晚餐？

What time will dinner be served？

我討厭飛機食物。

I hate airplane food.

供應飲料的推車會很快過來嗎？

Will the drink cart come around soon？

麻煩一下,我要去咖啡因的。

Decaf, please.

3 請給我一條毛毯

May I have a blanket, please?

請給我一條毛毯好嗎？

一個枕頭

a pillow

耳機

ear phones

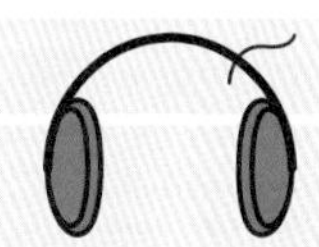

一份中文報紙

a Chinese newspaper

免稅商品目錄

the duty-free catalogue

小孩子可以玩的東西

something for my kids to play with

嘔吐袋

the vomit bag

遮光眼罩

eyemask

4 請問，廁所在哪裡

Excuse me, where is the bathroom?

對不起，請問廁所在哪裡？

洗手間

the lavatory

商務客艙

business class

我的安全帶

my seat belt

閱讀燈

the reading light

逃生門

the emergency exit

救生衣

life vest

例句

我的旅行袋放不進去。

My bag won't fit.

對不起。

Excuse me.

我可以跟你換位子嗎？

Can I switch seats with you？

我可以把椅子放下來嗎？

Can I recline my seat？

對不起，麻煩你把椅子拉上，謝謝。

Excuse me, can you put your seat up, please？

這是免費的嗎？

Is this free？

洛杉磯幾點？

What time is it in Los Angeles？

您說什麼？

Pardon me？

上午7點40分。

It's seven forty a.m.

飛機上要播放哪一部電影？

What movies will you be showing on this flight？

我可以坐在緊急出口處的那排座位嗎？

Can I sit in an exit row？

我想要有更多空間把腳伸直。

I like the extra leg room.

我們今天的飛行時間有多長？

What is our flying time today？

可以請你打開空調氣孔嗎？

Could you please open the air vent？

你不可以在飛機上抽煙。

You can't smoke on the airplane.

請問我可以借你的筆嗎?

May I borrow your pen, please?

小小專欄

☆飛機上的廁所寫的是“**lavatory**”，若使用中則顯示“**occupied**”，若無人使用，則為vacant。

☆**[Excuse me]**表示「打擾了」、「勞駕」的意思，一般用在為了引起他人注意或因為可能打擾他人，如打斷別人的談話、在人群中推擠到別人或不同意別人的意見等。

☆**[Pardon me？（↗）]**如果語調是上揚的，表示聽不清楚（聽不到）或不瞭解對方說的，請求對方再說一次；如果語調是下降的，那麼意思跟上面的**[Excuse me]**一樣。

☆時間的說法可以省略小時、分鐘，例如，7點40分直接說成“**seven forty**”或“**twenty to eight**”；12點15分說成“**twelve fifteen**”或“**a quarter past twelve**”；5點半說成“**five thirty**”或“**thirty past five**”。還有，時間後面記得加上a.m.（上午）、p.m.（下午）喔！

5 跟鄰座乘客聊天

A **Can you speak nglish?**

你會說英文嗎？

B **—Yes, a little.**

—是的，一點點。

日文	中文	德文	西班牙文
Japanese	**Chinese**	**German**	**Spanish**

台語	法文	義大利文
Taiwanese	**French**	**Italian**

例句

我正在學習中。

I'm learning.

我的英文不太好。

My English is not good.

你要去哪裡？

Where are you going?

是的，現在是到西雅圖旅行的最好時間。

Yeah, it's the best time to visit Seattle.

你是為了公事出差還是休閒旅遊？

Are you traveling for business or for pleasure？

我希望我可以去澳洲渡個假。

I wish I could take a vacation to Australia.

你不喜歡飛機上的食物嗎？
Don't you just love airplane food？

你有小孩嗎？
Do you have any kids？

我兒子在美國讀書。
My son is studying in the States.

你來自歐洲嗎？
Are you from Europe？

你是從事那個行業？
What do you do？

這是你第一次到澳洲嗎？
Is this your first time to visit Australia？

是的！我很興奮去那裡。
Yes, it is. I'm so excited to go there.

能和你交談感覺真好。
Oh, It's been nice talking to you.

你也是。
You, too.

祝你日本之旅愉快。
Enjoy your trip to Japan.

小小專欄

☆[I wish I could take a vacation to Australia.]中的"vacation"指一段較長時間的休假、假期時間；而"holiday"是指因為節日或慶祝而放假的短期假日。

不想和旁人講話時

旅途遙遠，我需要睡一下。
Well, it's a long flight, I need to get some sleep.

我想看的電影開始播放了。
Oh! The movie I want to watch is on.

我真的需要看完這本書。

I really need to finish this book.

對不起，但是我真的很累了。

Sorry, but I'm pretty tired.

如果你不介意的話，我想要睡覺了。

If you don't mind, I'm going to close my eyes now.

不好意思，我必需寫一封信。

Excuse me, I have to write a letter.

6 我是來觀光的

A What is the purpose of your visit?

你旅行的目的為何？

B —Sight-seeing.

—觀光。

讀書

For study

商務

Business

探親

Visiting relatives

拜訪朋友

Visiting friends

小小專欄

[for study]中的“study”(學習)強調學習的過程，帶有深入的研讀並將所學之事物融會貫通之意。另一個字“learn”(學習）是透過學習而得到某種知識或是技術，強調學會這個結果。

7 我住達拉斯的假期酒店

A **Where will you stay?**

你會待在哪裡？

B —**At the Holiday Inn in Dallas.**

—達拉斯的假期酒店。

和朋友住
With my friends

和家人
With family

和同事
With my colleague

在希爾頓飯店
At the Hilton

在學校的宿舍
In the school dorms / dormitory

例句

你有朋友的地址嗎？

Do you have your friend's address？

我現在身上沒有帶地址。

I don't have the address with me now.

我朋友住在芝加哥。

My friend lives in Chicago.

我不太會說英文。

I don't speak English well.

我兒子會在甘迺迪機場接我。

My son will pick me up at JFK Airport.

是的，這就是飯店的地址。

Yeah, the address of the hotel is here.

租車服務台在哪裡？

Where are the car rental agencies？

旅館有提供小型巴士載客服務嗎？

Does the hotel have a van？

距離最近的付費電話在哪裡？

Where is the nearest payphone？

每小時一班到市中心的公車站在哪？

Where is the bus stop for the hourly shuttle to the center?

小小專欄

☆九一一攻擊事件之後，美國的海關會要求旅客填寫停留的地址。

8 我停留十四天

A How long will you stay?

你會停留多久呢？

B —14 days.

—十四天。

只有五天	一個禮拜
Only five days	A week
大概兩個禮拜	一個月
About two weeks	A month
大概十天	半年
About ten days	Half a year

9 我要換錢

我想兌換五千台幣，謝謝你。

I want to exchange 5000 NT dollars, please.

現在的兌幣匯率是多少？

What is the exchange rate？

旅行支票兌現，麻煩你。

I'd like to cash a traveler's check, please.

台幣換成美金。

From NT to US dollars.

台幣換成歐元。

From NT to Euros.

你可以把一百元換成小鈔嗎？

Can you break a hundred？

麻煩你給我一些小鈔。

Small bills, please.

手續費是多少錢？

How much is the commission？

請在這裡簽名。

Please sign here.

護照，麻煩你。

Passport, please.

這是我的護照。

Here is my passport.

可以請你開給我收據嗎？

Can I have a receipt, please？

請問你有信封嗎？

Do you have an envelope？

10 您有需要申報的東西嗎？

A **Would you open your bag, please? What's this?**

麻煩你把袋子打開。這是什麼？

B **—It's my camera.**

—這是我的照相機。

化妝品

make-up

胃藥

medicine for my stomach

安眠藥

bottle of sleeping pills

筆記型電腦

lap-top computer

給我孫子的禮物

gift for my grandson

小小專欄

☆帶藥進美國，要將藥劑放在原處方的罐子裡，否則需要出示醫生證明

例句

先生，有需要申報的東西嗎？

Anything to declare, sir？

你想要檢查多少個旅行袋？

How many bags do you want to check？

你有多少行李？

How many pieces of luggage do you have？

我可以在哪裡拿到行李推車？

Where can I get a luggage cart？

行李領取處在哪裡？

Where is the baggage claim？

失物招領處在哪裡？

Where is the lost and found？

詢問處理遺失行李的櫃檯在哪裡？

Where is the lost luggage counter？

我想我的背包已經壞掉了。我該怎麼申請賠償？

I think my bag has been damaged. How can I file for compensation？

我該去哪裡通過海關檢查？

Where can I go through customs？

好的，你現在可以離開了。

OK, you can go, now.

好用單字

手提行李

carry-on bag

超重

overweight

經濟客艙

economy class

商務客艙

business class

頭等艙

first class

檢查

check

機場服務中心

Airport Information Center

公事包

briefcase

11 轉 機

轉機服務台在哪裡？

Where is the transfer desk ?

我要過境到達拉斯。

I need to transit to Dallas.

班機何時出發？

When will the flight depart ?

登機時間是何時？

What's the boarding time ?

16號登機門在哪裡？

Where is Gate No. 16 ?

我該如何去第三航廈？

How do I get to Terminal 3 ?

我的背包必須再檢查一次。

I need to recheck my bags.

我需要新的登機證嗎？

Do I need a new boarding pass ?

飛機幾點會到達達拉斯？

What time does that flight arrive in Dallas ?

請問你們有早一點的班機嗎？

Do you have an earlier flight ?

請問你們有直航的班機嗎？

Do you have a direct flight ?

我需要再辦登機手續嗎?

Do I need to check in again ?

12 怎麼打國際電話

對不起，你有一元的零錢嗎？

Excuse me, do you have change for a dollar？

撥打本地電話是多少錢？

How much is a local call？

35分錢可以打幾分鐘的電話？

35 ¢ for how many minutes ?

你可以教我怎麼打電話嗎？

Can you show me how to make a phone call ?

首先撥"0"接線員會幫你服務。

Just dial "0". The operator will help you.

我可以打一通國際對方付費的電話嗎？

Can I make an international collect call ?

請問哪裡有在賣長途電話卡？

Where do they sell long-distance phone cards ?

這附近有公共電話嗎？

Is there a public phone around here ?

要怎麼打對方付費國際電話？

How do you make a collect call ?

我想要打一通對方付費的電話。

I'd like to make a collect call.

我可以使用我的電話卡嗎？

Can I use my calling card ?

打到倫敦的區域號碼幾號?

What is the dialing code for London?

小小專欄

☆[make a collect call]是指對方付費的國際電話。而國際電話叫[international call]。至於電話號碼的說法是[My telephone number is 3456789]數字的說法是[three, four,five-six, seven, eight, nine]。

13 我要打市內電話

喂！

Hello？

嗨！我是南希，包伯在家嗎？

Hi. This is Nacy. Is Bob there？

他剛剛外出。

He just stepped out.

那麼請你轉告他，我來電過待會兒再打給他。

Would you please tell him that I called and I'll call back later？

好的，我會轉告他的。

Ok. I'll give him the message.

我打錯電話了。

I've got the wrong number.

小小專欄

☆打電話對方不在，希望對方代為傳話就用 **[Would you please tell…that…]**這樣的說法。拜託別人代為傳達事情放在**“That”**的後面。

美國錢幣介紹

一元鈔票

a dollar bill

1便士

a penny: 1 ¢

五分錢

a nickel: 5 ¢

10分錢

a dime: 10 ¢

2角5分

a quarter: 25 ¢

五角銀幣

a fifty-cent piece: 50 ¢

一元硬幣

one-dollar coin: $1.00

五元紙鈔

five- dollar bill: $5.00

14 請給我一份市區地圖

A city map, please?

請給我一份市區地圖。

MAP

紐約市導覽
A New York City Guide

一日遊資訊
One-day Tour Info

滑雪行程資訊
Skiing Tour Info

公車路線說明
Bus routes

市區酒店清單
A list of hotels downtown

觀光指南
A tourist guide

小小專欄

"**map**"地圖，指各種因為不同目標而製作的單張地圖。還有另一個字"**atlas**"，是把許多相關 的地圖，集結成冊的地圖集。

1 我要訂一間單人房

二、飯店

I want to reserve a single room.
我要預約單人房。

雙人床	兩張床
a twin room	a double room
四人房間	附淋浴的房間
a four-person room	a room with a shower
附冷氣的房間	可以看到海的房間
a room with air-conditioning	a room with an ocean view
禁煙房間	雙人床三個晚上
a non-smoking room	a double for 3 nights

序數的說法

一	二	三	四
first	second	third	fourth
五	六	二十一	三十
fifth	sixth	twenty-first	thirtieth

2 我要住宿登記

我叫陳明。
My name is Chen Ming.

我有預約。
I have a reservation.

我沒有預約。
I don't have a reservation.

我今晚要住宿。
I need a room for the night.

有空房間嗎？
Do you have a room available？

我們有訂房，名字是陳明。
We have a reservation under Chen Ming. That's C-H-E-N M-I-N-G.

我們何時可登記入住？
When can we check in？

我現在可以住宿登記嗎？
Can I check in now？

包含早餐嗎？
Is breakfast included？

電梯在哪裡？
Where is the elevator？

你可以給我飯店的號碼嗎？
Can you give me the hotel's number？

一晚住宿是多少錢？
How much for one night？

還有更便宜的房間嗎？
Are there any cheaper rooms？

你有大一點的房間嗎？
Do you have a bigger room？

三個人可住在同一間房間嗎？

Can three people stay in a room？

退房是幾點？

When is the checkout time？

普通客房是$85，景觀客房是$100。

Regular rooms are $85. A room with a view is $100.

你們的房間裡可以收到有線電視嗎？

Do you have cable？

房間裡可以上網嗎？

Do the rooms have internet access？

這裡有客人使用的游泳池嗎？

Is there a pool for the guests to use？

這裡有健身俱樂部嗎？

Is there a health club？

如果可以的話我想要一間套房。

I would like a suite if one is avaliable.

3 我要客房服務

有提供客房服務嗎？

Do you have room service？

客房服務您好，有什麼我可以效勞的嗎？

Room Service, May I help you？

這裡是503號房。我想要點早餐。

Yes, This is room 503. I'd like to order some breakfast.

你們有洗衣服務嗎？

Do you have laundry service？

我想打市內電話。

I want to make a local call.

我想打長途電話。

I want to make a long-distance call.

我想打國際電話。

I want to make an international call.

我想寄明信片。

I'd like to send a postcard.

我要傳真。

I'd like to send a fax.

我可以用網路嗎？

Could I use the Internet？

我可以退房時一起算客房服務費嗎？

Can I pay the room service charge when I check out？

我要叫醒服務。

Wake-up call, please.

幾點叫醒您好呢？

What time would you like it？

早上六點。

At 6:00 a.m.

4 麻煩給我兩杯咖啡

Would you bring me two cups of coffee?

可以麻煩給我兩杯咖啡嗎？

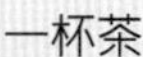

一杯茶

a cup of tea

一杯啤酒

a glass of beer

一壺熱開水
a pot of hot water

一些新鮮水果
some fresh fruit

5 我要吐司

I'd like toast.

我要吐司。

鬆餅
pancakes

培根
bacon

火腿加蛋
ham and eggs

比薩
pizza

三明治
a sandwich

臘腸
sausage

荷包蛋
fried eggs

6 房裡冷氣壞了

The TV in my room is broken.

我房間的電視壞了。

鎖
lock

暖氣
heater

迷你吧
mini-bar

按摩浴缸
Jacuzzi

冷氣
air conditioner

鬧鐘
alarm clock

吹風機
hair-drier

傳真
fax machine

Can I have a clean sheet, please?
我可以要一條乾淨的床單嗎？

一些衣架
some hangers

一些冰塊
some ice

枕頭

a pillow

一些乾淨的毛巾

some clean towels

熨斗

an iron

吹風機

a hair-drier

小小專欄

☆**[Can I have a clean sheet, please？]**中的“**Clean**”(乾淨）是形容處理得很乾淨、整齊，而沒有髒污的。另一個字“**clear**”(清晰）是形容視覺上的清晰、透明，或是清楚明白而有條理的。

例句

我把鑰匙忘在房裡了。

I left my key in the room.

我鑰匙丟了。

I've lost my key.

我不記得我的房號了。

I forgot my room number.

請換床單。

Please change the sheets.

廁所的水沖不下去。

The toilet doesn't flush well.

沒有毛巾。

There are no towels.

沒有衛生紙。

There's no toilet paper.

你可以教我怎麼用保險箱嗎？

Could you show me how to use the safe？

我可以換一個禁煙的房間嗎？

Can I change to a non-smoking room ?

請清掃我的房間。

Please clean up my room.

這是房間清理的服務嗎？

Is this housekeeping service ?

非常謝謝你。

Thank you very much.

請勿打擾。

Do not disturb.

可以請你馬上幫我處理嗎？

Can you please take care of it right away ?

好用單字

毛毯
blanket

肥皂
soap

棉被
comforter

床單
sheet

（電線）插頭
power outlet

插座
plug

床罩
bed spread

檯燈
lamp

水龍頭
faucet

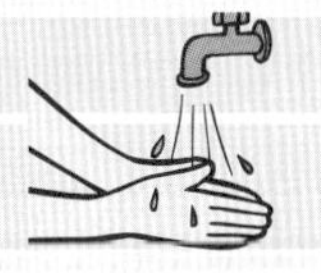

浴缸
bathtub

（櫃臺）保險櫃
safe deposit box

冰箱
refrigerator

健身房
gym

商務服務
business service

衣櫥
closet

游泳池
swimming pool

拉
pull

推
push

緊急出口
Fire Exit

小小專欄

☆ **"business service"**（商務服務）是大型飯店中，專門提供上班族進行秘書及翻譯等工作。裡面還提供上網、傳真及打電話等服務。

7 我要退房

我想退房。
I want to check out.

我將在幾分鐘後退房。
I'll be checking out in a few minutes.

我很急。
I'm in a hurry.

麻煩你請人幫忙我拿行李好嗎？
Can you send someone up for my luggage, please？

請問我可以延長我的住房天數嗎？

Is it possible for me to extend my stay？

我覺得這裡可能有些錯誤。

I think there might be a mistake.

這一項是什麼？

What is this entry for？

我沒使用迷你吧。

I didn't use the mini-bar.

我沒有叫客房服務。

I didn't order room service.

這已包括稅金嗎？

Is this including tax？

請問你們接受現金嗎？

Do you accept cash？

你們接受信用卡嗎？

Do you accept credit cards？

我可以要一張收據嗎？

Can I have a receipt, please？

請問你可以幫我安排到機場的計程車嗎？

Could you arrange a taxi to the airport for me？

我在這裡住宿的很愉快。

I had a pleasant stay.

我可以看一下帳單嗎？

Can I check the bill?

小小專欄

[I'll be checking out in a few minutes.]中的“a few”是修飾可數名詞，表示一下下、一點點、不多之意。後接複數型態；相對地，“a little”修飾不可數名詞，表示一點點、不多。後接單數型態。

三、用 餐

附近有義大利餐廳嗎

Is there an Italian restaurant around here?

附近有義大利餐廳嗎？

日式餐廳

a Japanese restaurant

墨西哥餐廳

a Mexican restaurant

印度餐廳

an Indian restaurant

中國餐廳

a Chinese restaurant

韓國餐廳

a Korean restaurant

越南餐廳

a Vietnamese restaurant

印尼餐廳

an Indonesian restaurant

泰國餐廳

a Thai restaurant

義大利餐廳

an Italian restaurant

西班牙餐廳

a Spanish restaurant

法國餐廳

a French restaurant

希臘餐廳

a Greek restaurant

必勝客

a Pizza Hut

Subway

a Subway

速食餐廳

a fast food restaurant

例句

他們有海鮮嗎？
Do they have seafood？

那裡的菜好吃嗎？
Is the food good there？

那裡有什麼特別？
What's good there？

它在哪裡？
Where is it？

你推薦些什麼？
What do you recommend？

那很貴嗎？
Is it expensive？

你覺得酒單的內容如何呢？
How is the wine list？

那裡的氣氛怎麼樣？
What's the atmosphere like？

小小專欄

☆“dinner”是「晚餐、正餐」的意思，一般指晚餐。因為“dinner”是一天中最重要的一餐，而這一餐通常在晚上進行。但是為了假日、生日或某些特別的日子，精心烹製的豐盛膳食，常在中午或晚上舉行，這被稱做正餐。另外，“supper”是指簡便的晚餐或睡前吃的宵夜。如果午餐用“dinner”，就會將晚餐稱做“supper”。

2 我要預約

I want to make a reservation for 2 people at 6:00 tonight.
我要預約兩人今晚六點。

八人 / 今晚七點
8 people / 7:00 tonight

四人 / 明晚約八點
4 people / 8:00 tomorrow night

兩人 / 週六晚上六點
2 people / 6:00 on Saturday night

兩大人和一小孩 / 7月7日十二點
2 adults and 1 child / 12:00 on July 7th

例句

套餐多少錢？
How much is the set meal？

有沒有吸煙區？
Is there a smoking section？

有沒有靠窗的位子？
Can we have a table by the window？

有。
Yes.

沒有。

No.

有的，請您穿西裝繫領帶。

Yes, please wear a jacket and a tie.

可以讓寵物進去嗎？

Are pets allowed？

你們幾點停止供餐的服務？

What time do you stop serving？

我們要怎麼去餐廳？

How do we get to your restaurant？

你們有規定要穿禮服嗎？

Do you have a dress code？

不，我們不用。

No, we don't have one.

我們要等多久？

How long is the wait？

這裡該付 分之六的小費還是更多？

Is there a gratuity added to parties of 6 or more？

小小專欄

☆**[Can we have a table by the window？]**中的"**by**"指兩個物體之間緊緊的靠著，且無法在其中放入其他任何東西。另外，"**near**"指兩者之間的距離靠的很近，但距離比"**by**"來得遠。

好用單字

加高座椅	高腳椅	高腳凳	餐廳內小房間
booster chair	**high chair**	**bar stool**	**booth**

3 我要點菜

我已準備好要點菜。

I'm ready to order.

麻煩你給我看一下菜單。

Can I see a menu, please？

你推薦些什麼呢？

What do you recommend？

要不要來點魚和馬鈴薯片？

How about some fish and chips？

你們有什麼沾醬？

What kind of dressing do you have？

你們有沒有其它不同的沙拉醬？

Do you have any different salad dressings？

我要這個。

This one, please.

我可以要一個小盤子嗎？

Can I have a small plate, please？

水就可以，謝謝。

Just water, thanks.

今天的特餐是甚麼？

What is today's special？

這條鮭魚新鮮嗎？

Is the salmon fresh？

請問你們有素食的主菜嗎？

Do you have any vegetarian entrees？

你們今天提供什麼晚餐呢？

What will you be having this evening？

你們有甜點的菜單嗎？

Do you have a dessert menu？

小小專欄

☆**[Can I have a small plate, please？]**中的“**plate**”是比較小而平的盤子，通常都是指放在每個人座位之前供自己使用的。而“**dish**”是泛指盤子，也可以專指盛裝菜餚，比較有深度的大盤子。

☆**[fish and chips]**是由英國傳入美國的食物，一般是把馬鈴薯片跟炸魚放在同一個盤子裡，烹調方法方便，東西也相當可口。美國人吃魚的種類並不多，所以多以簡單的一個“**fish**”來總稱。

4 你有義大利麵嗎？

Do you have spaghetti?

你有義大利麵嗎？

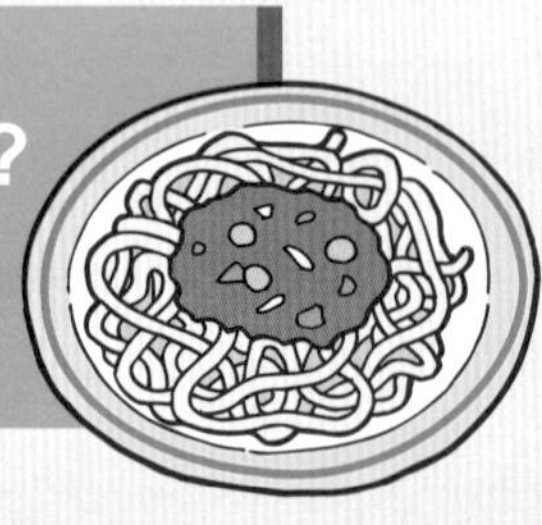

漢堡
hamburgers

牛肉麵
beef noodle soup

比薩
pizza

三明治
sandwich(es)

火鍋
hot pot

生魚片
sashimi

咖哩飯
curry rice

烤馬鈴薯
baked potatoes

韓國烤肉
Korean BBQ/ barbecues

5 給我火腿三明治

I'll have the ham sandwiches.

給我火腿三明治。

燉牛肉
beef stew

漢堡肉排
hamburg steak

蒸龍蝦尾
steamed lobster tail

烤鮭魚
grilled salmon

烤劍魚排	煎焗彩紅鱒魚
grilled swordfish steak	**pan-fried rainbow trout**
烤蝦&扇貝	烤馬鈴薯
grilled shrimp&scallops	**baked potato**

6 給我果汁

A **Would you like something to drink?**
要不要喝點飲料？

B **—Yes. I'd like <u>coffee</u>, please.**
—好，請給我<u>咖啡</u>。

果汁
juice

礦泉水
mineral water

茶
tea

熱可可
hot chocolate

可樂

Coke

冰沙

a smoothie

蘋果西打

apple cider

檸檬汽水

lemon fizz

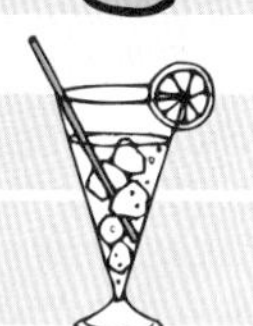

冰咖啡

iced coffee

濃縮咖啡

espresso

卡布奇諾

cappuccino

歐雷咖啡(拿鐵咖啡)

cafe au lait

檸檬茶

tea with lemon

奶茶

tea with milk

冰茶

iced tea

七喜

7up

事可樂

Pepsi

優格

yogurt

7 給我啤酒

A **What would you like to drink before dinner?**
餐前您想要喝些什麼嗎？

B —**Beer, please.**
—啤酒，麻煩你。

一杯葡萄酒
A glass of wine

自製的酒
House wine

威啤酒
Budweiser

一瓶啤酒
A bottle of beer

生啤酒
Draft beer

雪利酒
Sherry

白酒
White wine

紅酒
Red wine

白蘭地
Brandy

香檳
Champagne

薑汁汽水
Ginger ale

8 我還要甜點

A Do you want <u>some cake</u>?

你想要來點<u>蛋糕</u>嗎？

B —Sure!

—當然！

冰淇淋

some ice cream

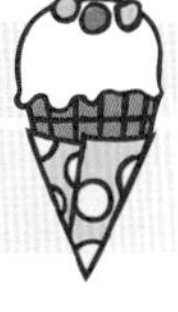

蘋果派

some apple pie

聖代

a sundae

香蕉奶昔

a banana milk shake

起司蛋糕

some cheesecake

櫻桃派

some cherry pie

巧克力蛋糕

some chocolate cake

覆盆子餡塔

some raspberry tart

鬆餅

a waffle

布朗尼(果仁巧克力)

a brownie

A Do you want some dessert ⁄drinks?

你想吃甜點（喝飲料）嗎？

B —Cheese cake, please.

—起司蛋糕，麻煩你。

冰淇淋

Ice cream

布丁

Pudding

馬芬

A muffin

司康

A scone

無咖啡因咖啡

Decaf coffee

冰摩卡咖啡

An iced-mocha

黑咖啡

Black coffee

只要糖，不要奶精

Sugar and no cream

義式濃縮咖啡

An espresso

例句

你們有餐巾嗎？

Do you have a napkin？

請回沖，謝謝。

I'd like a refill, please.

這是冰淇淋派嗎？

Is the pie a la mode？

可以再給我一些麵包嗎？

Some more bread, please？

可以幫我拿一下鹽嗎？

Could you pass the salt, please？

可以給我水嗎？

Can I have some water？

不好意思，我的叉子掉了。

Excuse me, I dropped my fork.

我可以要一個茶匙嗎？

Can I have a teaspoon？

我叫了咖啡，但是還沒有來。

I ordered coffee, but it hasn't come yet.

這個蛋糕真好吃，我一定要找到它的食譜。

This cake is delicious. I must get the recipe.

剩下的我可以帶走嗎？

Can I take home the rest？

您覺得餐點還好嗎？

Is everything all right?

9 吃牛排

A **How do you like your steak?**

你的牛排要幾分熟？

B —**Rare.**

—三分。

五分	七分	全熟
Medium	Medium-well	Well-done

好用單字

馬鈴薯泥	mashed potatoes
雞胸	chicken breast
小牛肉	veal
羊肉	mutton
龍蝦	lobster
大蝦	prawns
鮭魚	salmon
生蠔	oysters
沙朗牛排	sirloin
腓排	fillet
魚排	fish-fillet
鮪魚腓肋	tuna steak

10 墨西哥料理也不錯

脆塔可餅	法士達	辣椒起司薄片	墨西哥玉米脆片
taco	**fajita**	**nachos**	**chips**

墨西哥玉米薄餅	酪梨
tortillas	**avocado**

墨西哥點心	莎莎醬	起司
sopapillas	**salsa**	**queso**

小小專欄

☆墨西哥菜單上，皆是西班牙語，所以記得把**J**發成**H**的音，兩個**L**在一起不發音，點菜時就八九不離十了。

11 在早餐店

A **How do you want your eggs?**

你要怎樣料理你的雞蛋？

B —**Scrambled.**

—炒的。

單面煎	荷包蛋
Sunny-side up	**Over-easy**

半熟荷包蛋

over-medium

煮（生蛋整顆放到水裡煮熟）

boiled

水煮（生蛋去殼放到水裡煮熟）

poached

12 在速食店

I want a cheeseburger.

我要一個起司漢堡。

一個巨無霸漢堡

a Big Mac

一些雞塊

some chicken nuggets

一個魚排堡

a fish-fillet

一份大薯條

a large fries

一份蘋果派

an apple pie

一份冰淇淋

an ice cream

草莓聖代（巧克力／香草）

a strawberry sundae (chocolate / vanilla)

火雞肉三明治

a turkey sandwich

烤牛肉三明治

a roast beef sandwich

例句

內用或是外帶？

For here, or to go？

內用。

For here, please.

外帶。

Make it to go, please.

可樂要多大杯？

What size Coke would you like？

我要大（中／小）的。

Large(medium / small), please.

您要哪種麵包？

What kind of bread would you like？

您要放蕃茄醬嗎？

Would you like ketchup on it？

我不要洋蔥。

Without onions, please.

小小專欄

☆在美國的速食店裡，蕃茄醬"ketchup"及芥茉醬"mustard"都是放在一旁自行取用的。而飲料也是無限續杯的。

☆速食店裡的店員會問你[For here or to go？]意思是，內用或外帶。而"Drive Thru"就是車道點餐處。

13 付 款

我去拿帳單。
Let me get the bill.

我們各付各的吧。
Let's go dutch.

我來付帳。
It's on me.

我堅持這次由我來付帳。
It's my treat. I insist.

麻煩你，我要買單。
Can I have the bill, please？

在這裡付，還是在櫃台付？
Do I pay here or at the cashier？

一個馬芬和一杯拿鐵咖啡共是多少錢？
How much is a muffin and a latte？

這是什麼費用？
What is this charge for？

我們該付多少小費？
How much should we tip？

這有含稅嗎？
Is that including tax？

你們接受信用卡付費嗎？
Do you accept credit cards？

餐點真好吃。謝謝你！
I enjoyed the meal very much. Thank you.

小小專欄

在美國用餐，只要是有侍者（waiter）服務的餐廳或咖啡廳皆要付小費。若是現金付款，直接將小費放在桌上；若是以信用卡買單，則把小費(tips)的金額，填在簽帳單的小費（tips）欄裡。

四、購物

Is there a department store in this area?
這個地區有百貨公司嗎？

購物商場
shopping mall

雜貨店
grocery store

超級市場
supermarket

便利商店
convenience store

運動用品店
sporting goods store

書局
book store

唱片行
CD shop

藥局
pharmacy

花店
flower shop

精品店
boutique

鞋店

shoe store

珠寶店

jewelry store

古董店

antique store

美容沙龍

salon

美妝用品店

cosmetics store

紀念品商店

souvenir shop

二手衣專賣店

secondhand clothing store

2 女裝在哪裡

Where is women's wear?

女裝在哪裡？

男裝

men's wear

童裝

children's wear

化妝品部
the cosmetics department

家電
home appliances

藥品
the pharmacy

禮品包裝
gift-wrapping

服務台
the information desk

入口 / 出口
the entrance / exit

運動品部
the sporting goods department

小小專欄

☆[**gift-wrapping**]中的“**gift**”是指令人感到開心感動的禮物，偏重情感上的色彩，有包含送禮人的心意的意味。還有一個字“**present**”是指因為某些特定場合或是日子而贈送的禮品。

3 買小東西（1）

A May I help you?

有什麼我可以幫忙的嗎？

B —I'm looking for a digital camera.

—我在找數位相機。

鋼珠筆

a pen / ballpoint pen

筆記本

a notebook

書

a book

報紙

a newspaper

雜誌

a magazine

明信片

a postcard

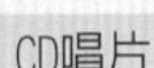

CD唱片

a CD

背包

a bag

帽子

a hat

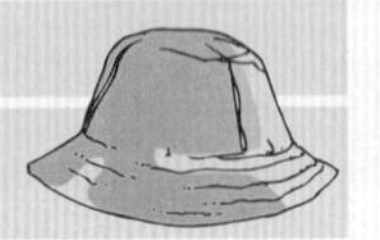

耳環

earrings

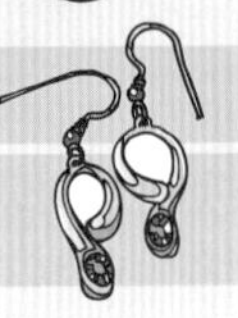

自來水筆
a fountain pen

隨身日記本
a pocket dairy

唱片
a record

領帶
a tie

世界知名品牌
world famous brands

配件
accessories

夾式耳環
clip-on earrings

戒指
a ring

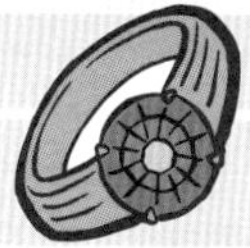

手鐲
a bracelet

鍊墜
a pendant

領帶夾
a tie pin

胸針
a brooch

鴨舌帽
a cap

香水
perfume

指甲油
nail polish

洗髮精
shampoo

潤絲精
conditioner

太陽眼鏡
sunglasses

防曬油
sunscreen

買小東西（2）

I'd like to buy a swimsuit.

我想要買泳衣。

比基尼
a bikini

燈具
a lighter

泳褲
swimming trunks

緊身衣褲
pantyhose

餐具
tableware

毛娃娃
a stuffed animal

煙斗
a pipe

皮夾
a wallet

精油蠟燭
an aromatic candle

花香料
potpourri

内衣褲
underwear

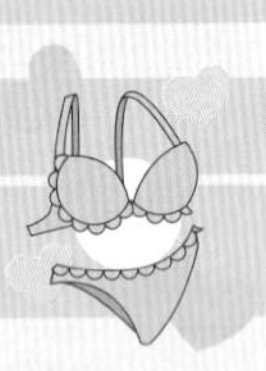

襪子
socks

手帕
a handkerchief

圍巾
a scarf

香菸
cigarettes

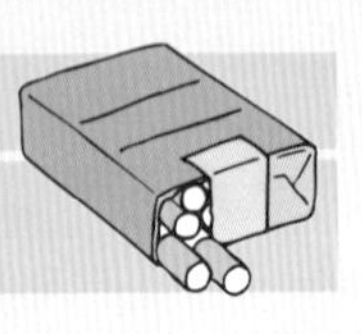

衛生棉
sanitary items

5 我要看毛衣

I'm looking for a sweater.

我要看毛衣。

西裝

a suit

連身裙

a dress

T-恤

a T-shirt

裙子

a skirt

睡衣

pajamas

牛仔褲

jeans

褲子

a pair of pants

手套

a pair of gloves

外套

a coat

夾克

a jacket

背心

a vest

游泳衣

a swimsuit

短上衣

a blouse

胸罩

a bra

領帶

a tie

毛巾

towels

6 買衣服

I'm looking for a T-shirt.

我正在找T恤。

夾克	馬球衫	休閒衫	套衫
jacket	polo shirt	casual shirt	pullover
胸前開釦的羊毛衫	牛仔夾克	外套	大尺碼
cardigan	jean jacket	coat	size large

洋裝
dress

襯衫
dress shirt

裙子
skirt

套裝
suit

衣服相關單字

長褲	牛仔褲	水手服	V領
trousers	jeans	crew neck	V-neck

圓領
turtle neck

短袖
short sleeve(shirt)

長袖
long sleeve(shirt)

三分袖
three-quarter-sleeve(shirt)

無袖
sleeveless(shirt)

聚酯棉紗
poly-cotton

棉
cotton

絲
silk

亞麻布
linen

聚酯纖維
polyester

7 店員常說的話

您要什麼？
May I help you？

這個如何？
What about this one？

這是知名品牌。
It's a well-known brand.

你穿起來很好看。
It looks nice on you.

它們真是完美的搭配。
They match perfectly.

它們是特價商品嗎？
Are they on sale？

樣式很流行。

It's in style.

這正好很合身。

It's a perfect fit.

你穿起來真好看。

It looks fabulous on you.

你穿起來真好看。

You look great in it.

小小專欄

☆[a pair of gloves pair]中的“pair”指成雙成對的物品，只要少了其中一個，就無法產生作用或是變得不完整的。相對地，還有一個字“couple”是指同一類的事物有兩個。雖然兩者之間有關係，可以聯繫在一起，但是分開後依舊具有其獨立 。

8 我可以試穿嗎

我可以試穿嗎？

Can I try it on？

我可以看看那個嗎？

Can I see that one, please？

你們有沒有別的顏色？

Do you have this in any other colors？

你穿起來很好看。

It looks nice on you.

很合身。

It fits well.

你可以照照鏡子。

You can take a look in the mirror.

試衣間在那裡？

Where's the fitting room？

不合身。

It doesn't fit.

你們的商品有可以換貨的服務嗎？

Do you do alterations？

你有「S」號的嗎？

Do you have a size"S"?

9 我要紅色那件

I want the red ones.

我要紅色的那件。

黃色

yellow

灰色

gray

橘色

orange

紅色

red

粉紅色

pink

白色

white

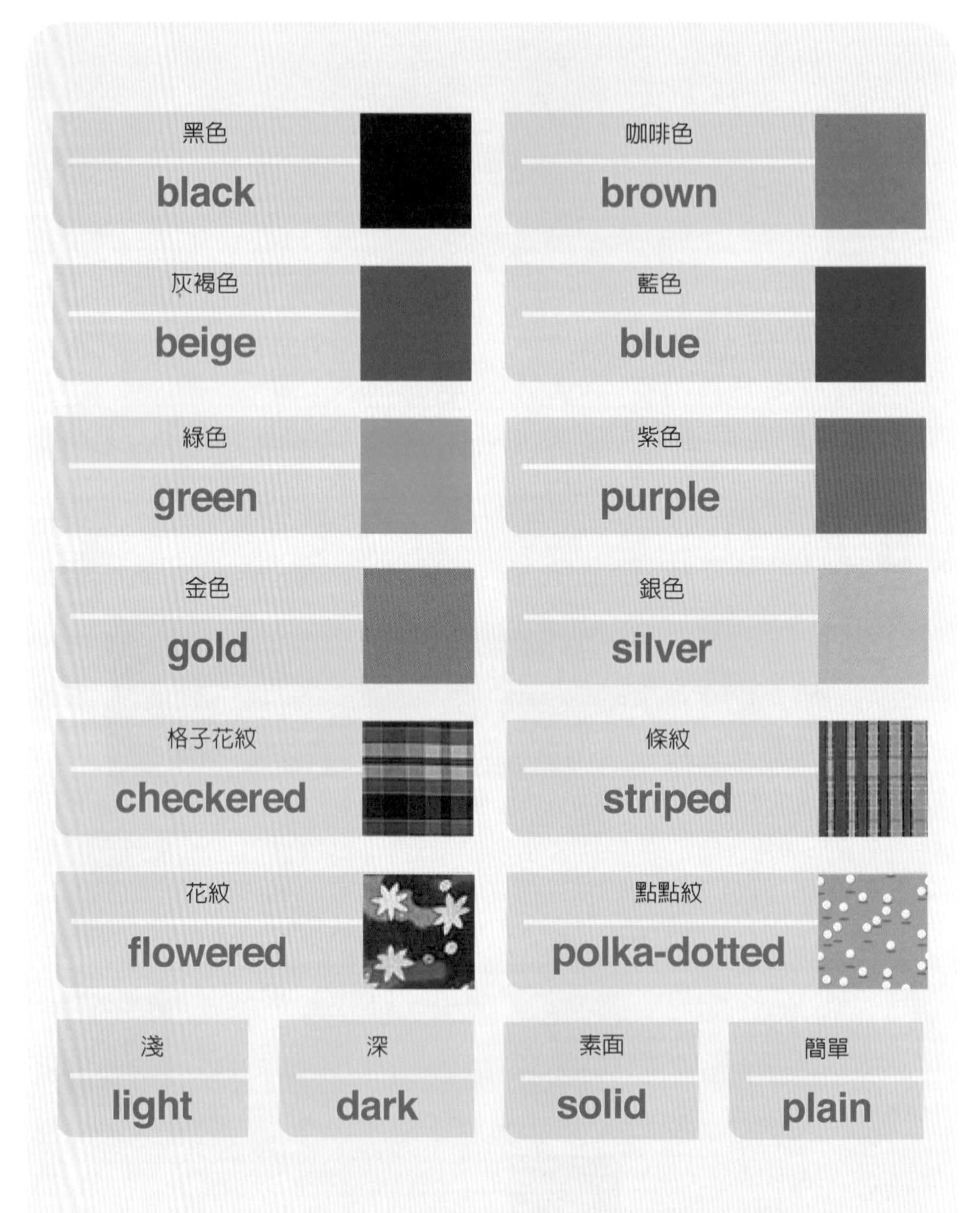
黑色
black
咖啡色
brown
灰褐色
beige
藍色
blue
綠色
green
紫色
purple
金色
gold
銀色
silver
格子花紋
checkered
條紋
striped
花紋
flowered
點點紋
polka-dotted
淺
light
深
dark
素面
solid
簡單
plain

10 這是棉製品嗎

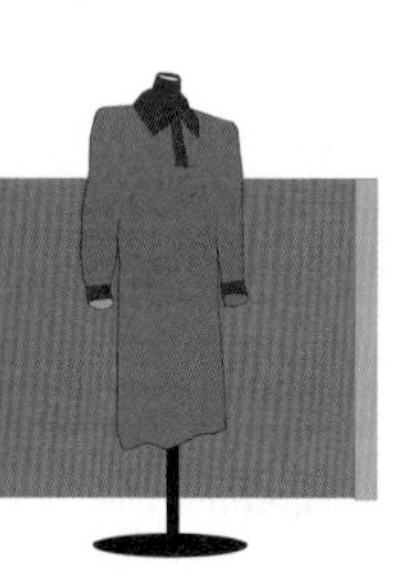

Is this cotton?

這是棉製品嗎？

亞麻布	尼龍	聚酯	絲
linen	**nylon**	**polyester**	**silk**
毛	皮	羊毛	山羊絨
fur	**leather**	**wool**	**cashmere**

11 我不喜歡那個顏色

I don't like the color.

我不喜歡那個顏色。

樣式	品質	材質	款式
pattern	**quality**	**material**	**style**

例句

穿起來很舒服。

It feels good.

這只能乾洗嗎？

Is it dry-clean only？

我能把它放進烘衣機嗎？

Can I put it in the dryer？

會縮水嗎？

Will it shrink？

會退顏色嗎？

Will the color fade？

能防水嗎？

Is this waterproof？

我能用洗衣機洗嗎？

Can I put it in the washing machine？

這要用手洗嗎？

Do I have to hand-wash this？

我要怎麼保養它？

How should I care for this？

可以掛到外面曬乾嗎？

Can I hang it out to dry？

12 太小了

It's too small.

太小了。

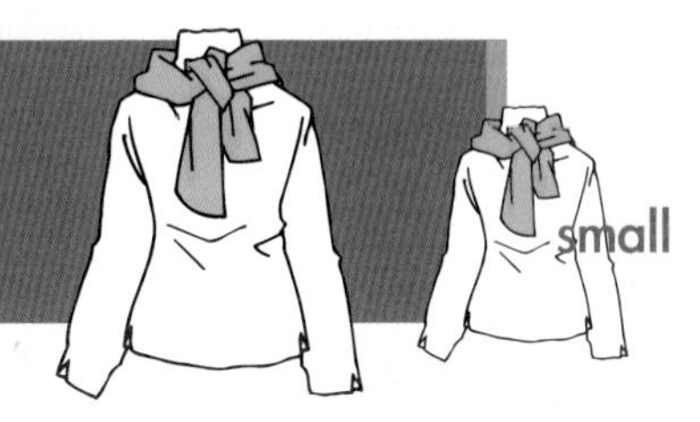

大	長	短	簡單
big	**long**	**short**	**plain**
貴	鬆	緊	硬
expensive	**loose**	**tight**	**hard**

例句

這件對我而言太小了。

It's too small for me.

你有沒有大一點的？

Do you have a bigger one？

這是大尺寸的。

Here is a size large.

我相信這件適合你穿。

I believe it will fit you.

這件適合我。

It fits me well.

你有「L」號的嗎？

Do you have a size"L"?

小小專欄

店員拿給我們的貨品，如果覺得太大、太小或是太貴，就可以說[It's too big (small, expensive)for me.]；剛好合身說[It fits me well.]。

13 我要這件

我喜歡這件。

I like this one.

我要這件。

I'll take this one.

你還要什麼嗎？

Do you need anything else？

這個也不錯。

This one is nice, too.

這個如何？

How about this one？

你要一條裙子來搭配你的新襯衫嗎？

Do you want a skirt to go with your new shirt？

14 你能改長一點嗎

Can you alter it? Make it a little <u>longer</u>, please.
你能修改一下嗎？麻煩你改<u>長</u>一點。

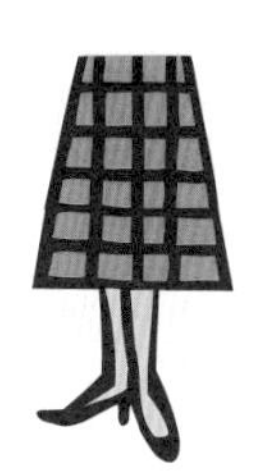

短一點	鬆一點	緊一點	大一點
shorter	**looser**	**tighter**	**bigger**

15 買鞋子

A How much are these <u>high heels</u>?
這雙<u>高跟鞋</u>多少錢？

B —They're $10.
—這個要十美元。

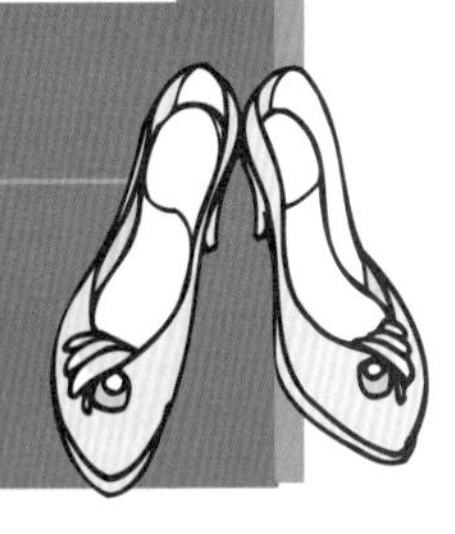

帆布運動鞋
sneakers

休閒鞋
loafers

女用搭配裙子的鞋子
dress shoes

拖鞋
mules

靴子
boots

西部靴
cowboy-boots

網球鞋
tennis shoes

慢跑鞋
jogging shoes

涼鞋
sandals

休閒鞋
hiking shoes

16 有大一點的嗎？

Do you have a larger size?

有大一點的嗎？

中碼
a medium

加大
an extra-large

小一點

a smaller size

更小一點

an extra small

小小專欄

☆[extra small]中的"small"是指客觀地以度量衡的標準，形容比較小的事物，含有經過比較而得的結果之意味。

有其他顏色嗎？

Do you have any in other colors?

有其他顏色嗎？

其他樣式

with other designs

其他材質

made from other material

其他花色

with another pattern

其他款式

other styles

18 我只是看看

我只是看看。

I'm just looking.

我打算繼續看看。

I'm going to keep looking.

也許就等下次吧。

Maybe next time.

我必須考慮一下。

I need to think about it.

也許不了。

Well, maybe not.

我待會再來。

I'll come back later.

謝謝，我只是看看而已。

Thanks. I'm only browsing.

謝謝！需要幫忙時我會叫你的。

Thank you. I'll let you know if I need any help.

19 物付錢

A How much is this?

這多少錢？

B —1,500 dollars.

—一千五 美元。

一分錢	五分錢	十分錢	二十五分錢
1 ¢	5 ¢	10 ¢	25 ¢

一元	五元	十元	二十元
$ 1	**$ 5**	**$ 10**	**$ 20**

五十元
$ 50

20 討價還價

對我而言太貴了。

It's too expensive for me.

算便宜一點嘛！

A little cheaper, please.

再打個折扣嘛！

A little discount, please.

二十美元的話就買。

If it costs less than $20, I could buy it.

他們這這禮拜特價中。

They're on special this week.

已經降到3美元了。

They've been reduced to 3 dollars.

這是半價了。

They're fifty percent off.

買兩個就送一個。

These are buy two, get the third one free.

小小專欄

☆**[on special=on sale]**（折價出售）。為了吸引顧客，店家總是挖空心思，做一些行銷策略，折價出售一些商品。在商品上用最醒目的字跟顏色大大寫上**“on sale”**或**“on special”**。逢年過節就更不用說了。

例句

收銀台在哪裡？

Where is the cashier？

這多少錢？

How much is this？

我還欠你多少錢？

How much do I owe you？

你少付我十元。

You are ten dollars short.

我要刷卡。

I'd like to pay by card.

您要分幾次付款？

How many installments？

一次。

One.

六次。

Six.

我可以付台幣嗎？

Can I pay in Taiwan dollar？

可以幫我寄到台灣嗎？

Could you ship this to Taiwan？

運費多少錢？

How much is the shipping cost？

什麼時候送到？

When will it arrive？

21 退貨換貨

我要退貨。

I'd like to return this.

我想換貨。

I'd like to exchange this.

我昨天買的。

I bought this yesterday.

我可以換別的東西嗎？

Can I exchange it for something else？

這裡有污漬。

There's a stain.

這裡有個洞。

There's a hole.

不合身。

It doesn't fit.

它讓我看起來很胖。

It makes me look fat.

我考慮很久了。

I'm having second thoughts.

我想退錢。

I'd like a refund.

這是收據。

Here's the receipt.

我們無法退錢。

It's nonrefundable.

五、各種交通

1 坐車去囉

A **Let's go by bus.**

去搭巴士吧。

B **—Ok.**

—好。

腳踏車	bike
汽車	car
捷運	MRT
電車	train
地鐵	subway
公車	bus
計程車	taxi
摩托車	motorcycle/ Amotorscooter
輪船	ship
飛機	airplane
船	boat
直升機	helicopter

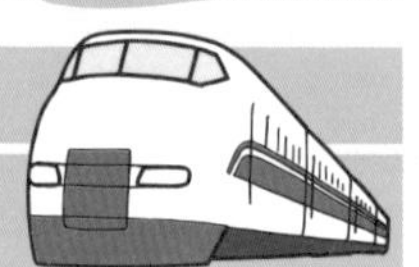

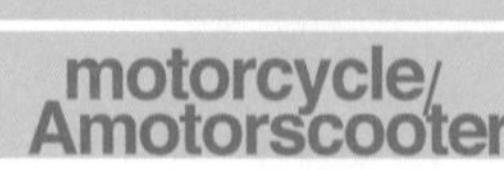

2 我要租車

A Do you have any compact cars?

請問你們有小型車嗎？

B —Of course.

—當然有。

省油的	中型的
economy	mid-sized
全套的	日本的
full-sized	Japanese
四門的	美國的
4-door	American

例句

總共多少錢？
What is the total?

有包括稅金跟保險費嗎？
Does it include tax and insurance?

我希望投所有的保險。
I'd like full coverage.

我的車子故障了。
My car broke down.

我的爆胎了。

I got a flat tire.

幫我叫拖車。

Please call a tow truck.

煞車不怎麼靈光。

The brakes don't work very well.

我不會開手排車。

I can't drive a stick.

你有自動排檔車嗎？

Do you have any automatics?

我不想租SUV。

I don't want to rent an SUV.

小小專欄

☆ **"stick"**是裝有手動變速器的汽車；**"automatic"**是裝有自動變速器的汽車。另外要提醒的是，在國外如果車子故障了，為了安全起見，請務必待在車內等待救援喔！

好用單字

駕照

driver's license

國際駕照

international driving permit

車子的種類

type of car

租車契約

rental contract

（車子）登記書

registration

先買票

去市中心的車票是多少錢？

How much is a ticket to downtown?

來回票

round-trip ticket

單程票

one-way ticket

多少錢？

How much is it?

要花多少時間？

How long does it take?

坐公車比較便宜嗎？

Is it cheaper to go by bus?

你要幾張車票？

How many tickets do you want?

我要買一張。

I'd like to buy a ticket.

我需要坐在指定的座位嗎？

Do I need to sit in an assigned seat?

對不起，我想這是我的座位。

Excuse me, I think you're in my seat.

小小專欄

☆**[downtown]**在美國是指位於都市市中心，有高樓大廈、 物中心等人群聚集、熱鬧的地方。順便一提，**"City"**（城市）通常是指人口密集度較高的都會區或城市；**"town"**（小鎮）是比城市的規模要小的鄉鎮；**"village"**（村落）常用來指以農業為主的小型聚落。

坐公車

公車站在哪裡？

Where is the bus stop ?

你們會停西八街嗎？

Do you stop at West 8th Street?

車票多少錢？

How much is the fare?

去西八街要多久？

How long does it take to West 8th Street?

看交通狀況而定。

It depends on the traffic.

我會說出你要下車的站名。

I'll call out your stop.

我要在這裡下車。

I'd like to get off here.

可以給我巴士路線圖嗎?

Can I have a bus route map?

不，請你坐104。

No, take the 104.

哪一輛公車會到那裡？

Which bus goes there?

104號公車來了。

Here comes the number 104 now!

我該下車時請你告訴我好嗎？

Will you tell me when to get off ?

請給我車票。

May I have a transfer ticket?

請開後車門。

Open the rear door, please.

請坐下。

Please sit down.

請坐我的位子。

Please take my seat.

小小專欄

☆不知道應該搭幾號公車到想去的地方，就說 **[Which bus goes there?]**。**[Here comes...]**是「你看！…來了」。想下車的時候，就拉“**Bell Code**”（下車鈴），其實看看其他乘客的作法就會啦！

好用單字

回數票
ticket book

一日遊票
one-day pass

目的地
destination

轉車
transfer

下一站
next stop

上車
get on

下車
get off

標記
token

閘門
gate

5 坐地鐵

Where is the subway station ?
地鐵站在哪裡？

入口	出口
entrance	**exit**

售票機	售票處
ticket machine	**fare adjustment office**

這火車有到中央公園嗎？
Does this train go to Central Park ?

有，有到。
Yes, it does.

沒到，你必須轉搭紅線。
No. You have to change to the Red line.

它有停中央公園嗎？
Will it stop at Central Park ?

到中央公園有幾站？
How many stops until Central Park?

我該到哪裡轉車？
Where do I transfer ?

下一班火車是何時到達？
When is the next train ?

我該在哪個站下車？
At which stop should I get off ?

我的車票不見了。
I lost my ticket.

不好意思，借過一下。
Would you let me pass, please ?

（讓位）請坐這裡。
You can have this seat.

謝謝你。
Thank you.

風景真好！
It's a wonderful view.

你要去哪裡？
Where are you going?

坐地鐵可以到很多地方。
You can get pretty much anywhere on the subway.

地鐵真方便。
The subway is really convenient.

好用單字

車票
ticket

回數券
coupon ticket

地鐵車票
a Metro Card

悠遊卡
a transit card

小小專欄

☆最近使用巴士跟公車通用的“**transit card**”（悠遊卡）的都市有增加的趨勢。

6 坐火車

去長島的車票。

A ticket to Long Island, please.

哪一天？

For what day?

今天，現在。

Today. Now.

五元。下一班火車在十點四十分開出。

That's five dollars. The next train leaves at 10:40.

小小專欄

☆[That's five dollars. The next train leaves at 10:40.]中的“leave”離開某地要出發前往另一個地方。另一個字，“Start”（開始）表示事情或是 作的開始或開端。

好用單字

（每站都停）普通車

local

快車

express

特快車

limited express

長途公車

coach

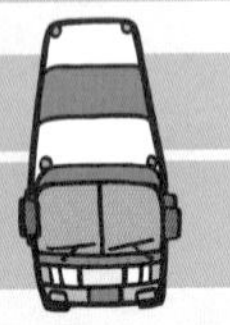

臥車

sleeping car

普通臥舖（2人臥舖個人房）

standard bedroom

車廂（有舒適座位及小吃的）	club car
車室	compartment
單程車票	one-way ticket
來回車票	round trip ticket
票價	train fare
時間表	timetable
候車室	waiting room
小吃車廂	dining car
讀書燈	reading light
車上行李架	luggage rack
來回旅程	round-trip
單程	one-way
驗票口	ticket barrier
車站	station
售票機	ticket machine
月台	platform
車軌	track
終點站	terminal

7. 坐計程車

去那裡？
Where to ?

173東85街。
173 East 85th Street.

我要到這個地址。
Please take me to this address.

到大中央車站要多久？
How long is the ride to Grand central Station?

到市中心計程車費要多少？
How much is the cab fare to downtown?

你可以讓我在這裡下車。
You can let me out here.

不必找錢了。
Keep the change.

就停在這裡吧。
Just pull over here.

你可以先停在梅西百貨嗎？
Can you stop by Macy's first?

這就是了。
This is it.

到了。
Here it is.

你可以搖下車窗嗎？
Can you roll down the window ?

可以開慢點嗎？
Could you please slow down a little ?

有沒有其它的路線？
Are there any alternate routes ?

可以給我收據嗎？

Can I have a receipt ?

你找的零錢不對。

You gave me the wrong change.

可以麻煩開後車廂嗎？

Could you open the trunk, please?

小小專欄

☆[173 East 85th Street.]中的"Street"（街道）指連接各鄉鎮、城市之間的道路。一般道路兩側建築物林立，包括車道跟步道；而"road"（路），泛指連接各城市、鄉鎮之間車子跑的道路；另外"path"（小徑），指鄉村或是山中讓人們方便通行的非正式道路。

好用單字

紅綠燈
traffic light

人行道
sidewalk

道路標誌
road sign

標誌
sign

鎖
block

地下道
underpass

8 糟糕！我迷路了

我迷路了。
I think I'm lost.

對不起，你可以告訴我車站在那裡嗎？
Excuse me. Can you show me where the bus station is ?

你可以告訴我正確的方向嗎？
Can you point me in the right direction?

我該怎麼去SOHO區呢？
How can I get to SOHO ?

我想到王子大廈。
I want to go to the Prince's Building.

很遠嗎？
Is it far?

有多遠呢？
How far is it?

從這裡到那裡只隔兩個街區。
It's only a couple of blocks from here.

這條路直走。
Go straight down this street.

這條路走約50公尺。
Go down this street about fifty meters.

在第二個紅綠燈右轉。
Turn right at the second traffic light.

在第二個轉角左轉。
Turn left at the second corner.

過橋後左轉。
Go across the bridge and take a left.

就在右邊。
It's on the right side.

一直往前走，你一定找得到的。

Go along and you're sure to get there.

從這到那裡很遠。

It's far from here.

你得坐公車。

You should go by bus.

請告訴我怎麼去。

Tell me how to get there, please.

你有地圖嗎？

Do you have a map ?

請幫我畫個地圖。

Draw a map for me, please.

謝謝你！

Thanks a lot.

我帶你去。

Come along with me.

小小專欄

☆[**Can you show me where the bus station is？**]中的“**show**”是用肢體表演或是親身示範，而使對方更清楚的理解。另外，美國的街道的劃分是以“**blocks**”跟“**streets**”來表示。“**block**”對我們來講比較陌生，它是指四面被街道包圍的一個街區單位。

9 其它道路指引說法

就在火車站旁邊

next to the train station

就在路口

at the corner

就在下一個十字路口

at the next intersection

在你左手邊

on your left-hand side

在梅西百貨和維珍唱片之間

between Macy's and Virgin Records

過那個紅綠燈

past that traffic light

在第三個路口右轉

turn right at the third corner

直走兩個街區

go straight 2 blocks

六、觀光

在旅遊諮詢中心

Could I have a sightseeing map, please?

請給我觀光地圖。

公車路線圖	地鐵路線圖
a bus route map	**a subway route map**

餐廳資訊	物資訊
a restaurant guide	**a shopping guide**

2 有一日遊嗎

Do you have a full-day tour?

你有一日遊嗎？

半天	晚上
a half day	**a night**

例句

旅遊諮詢中心在哪裡？

Where is the tourist information center?

你有滑雪之旅嗎？

Do you have a tour for skiing?

什麼時候開門？

When is it open?

博物館今天有開嗎？

Is the museum open today?

你能推薦好餐廳嗎？

Can you recommend a good restaurant?

你知道去哪裡參加旅遊團嗎？

Do you know where to join a tour?

他們有沒有講中文的導遊？

Do they have a Chinese-speaking guide?

博物館的入場費要多少錢？

How much does admission to the museum cost?

博物館內有咖啡廳嗎？

Is there a cafe in the museum?

你有語音導覽嗎？

Do you have an audio guide?

遊覽車集合場所在哪裡？

Where is the pick-up point?

我們要預約明天的一日遊。

We'd like to reserve a day tour for tomorrow.

小小專欄

☆我們來比較 **[tour, trip, travel]**這三個字的不同：

tour:指一次去拜訪多個地方，做視察或短時間觀光的旅行。

trip:通常是指短期的旅行，到特定地點遊覽之後，便回程的小型旅行。

travel:指去比較遠的地方，並且花費較長時間的到遠方去旅行遊歷。

3 我要去迪士尼樂園

I want to go to Disney Land.

我要去 迪士尼樂園。

看／煙火表演

see / a fireworks display

登山／某處

go hiking / somewhere

去／跳蚤市場

go to / a flea market

看／老匯表演

see / a Broadway show

看／展覽

see / an exhibition

看／電影

see / a movie

看／籃球比賽

see / a basketball game

去／圖書館

go to / a library

去／溜冰

go / roller

參觀／博物館

visit / the museum

小小專欄

☆[a basketball game]中的“game”在美國指各種關於智力，或是“baseball,football”等後面有“ball”的體能比賽。至於“tennis,golf,boxing”等用“math”。也指非正式娛樂性質的競賽。

4 我要怎麼去艾菲爾鐵塔

I would like to go to the Eiffel Tower.

我要怎麼到（法國）艾菲爾鐵塔。

羅浮宮（法國）

The Louvre (France)

萬里長城（中國）

the Great Wall of China (China)

紫禁城（中國）

the Forbidden City (China)

金字塔（埃及）

the Great Pyramids of Giza (Egypt)

人面獅身像（埃及）

the Sphynx (Egypt)

泰姬瑪哈陵（印度）

the Taj Mahal (India)

澳洲大堡礁（澳洲）

the Great Barrier Reef (Australia)

雪梨歌劇院（澳洲）

the Sydney Opera House (Australia)

尼加拉 大瀑布（美國）

Niagra Falls (USA)

大峽谷（美國）

the Grand Canyon (USA)

自由女神（美國）

the Statue of Liberty(USA)

比薩斜塔（義大利）

the Leaning Tower of Pisa (Italy)

羅馬競技場（義大利）

the Rome Colosseum (Italy)

吳哥窟（柬埔寨）

Angkor Wat (Cambodia)

萬神廟（希臘）

the Pantheon (Greece)

好用單字

美術館

art museum

博物館

museum

物園

zoo

水族館

aquarium

公園

park

大廈

building

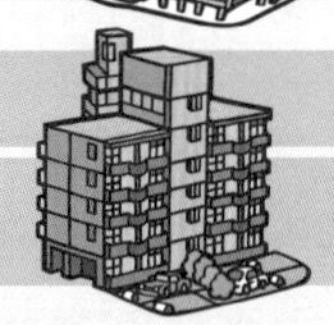

音樂廳

hall

圖書館

library

教堂

church

戲院、劇院

theatre

5 我想騎馬

I'd like to try <u>horseback riding</u>.
我想要去試試<u>騎馬</u>。

泛舟
rafting

滑翔翼
paragliding

熱氣球之旅
hot air balloon riding

跳傘
parachuting

深海潛水
scuba diving

高空彈跳
bungy jumping

滑雪
skiing

射擊
shooting

例句

我可以租釣魚用具嗎？
Can I rent fishing tackle?

腳踏車出租店在哪裡？
Where is the bicycle rental shop?

我可以租些裝備嗎？
Can I rent some equipment?

這是什麼樣的活動？
What kind of event is it?

在哪裡舉辦？
Where is it held?

幾點開始？
What time does it start?

小孩可以參加嗎？
Can children join ?

專車會送你回飯店。
The limousine will take you back to the hotel.

好用單字

高爾夫球場
golf course

海水浴場
beach

釣魚場
fishing spot

滑雪場
skiing resort

潛水場
diving spot

夜市
night market

跳蚤市場
flea market

高爾夫球具
golf clubs

滑雪用具
skiing outfit

潛水用具
diving gear

小小專欄

美國國定假日

New Year's Day

新年（一月一日）

Martin Luther King Day

馬丁·路德·金恩日（一月第三個星期一）

Presidents' Day

總統日（二月第三個星期一）

Memorial Day

陣亡將士紀念日（五月最後一個星期一）

Independence Day

獨立紀念日（七月四日）

Labor Day

勞工節（九月第一個星期一）

Columbus Day

哥倫布日（十月第二個星期一）

Veterans' Day

退伍軍人節（十一月十一日）

Thanksgiving Day

感恩節（十一月第四個星期四）

Christmas Day

聖誕節（十二月二十五日）

6 漫遊美國各州

A **Is this your first time to visit Ohio ?**

這是你第一次去俄亥俄州嗎？

B **—Yes.**

—對。

阿拉巴馬州	阿拉斯加州
Alabama (AL)	**Alaska (AK)**
亞利桑那州	阿肯色州
Arizona (AZ)	**Arkansas (AR)**
加利佛尼亞州	科羅拉多州
California (CA)	**Colorado (CO)**
康乃狄克州	德拉瓦州
Connecticut (CT)	**Delaware (DE)**
首都華盛頓	佛羅里達州
the District of Columbia (Washington, DC)	**Florida (FL)**
喬治亞州	關島
Georgia (GA)	**Guam**

夏威夷州
Hawaii (HI)

愛達荷州
Idaho (ID)

伊利諾州
Illinois (IL)

印地安那州
Indiana (IN)

愛荷華州
Iowa (IA)

堪薩斯州
Kansas (KS)

肯塔基州
Kentucky (KY)

路易斯安那州
Louisiana (LA)

緬因州
Maine (ME)

馬里蘭州
Maryland (MD)

麻薩諸塞州
Massachusetts (MA)

密西根州
Michigan (MI)

明尼蘇達州
Minnesota (MN)

密西西比州
Mississippi (MS)

密蘇里州
Missouri (MO)

蒙大拿州
Montana (MT)

內布拉斯加州	內華達州
Nebraska (NE)	**Nevada (NV)**
新罕布什爾州	新澤西州
New Hampshire (NH)	**New Jersey (NJ)**
新墨西哥州	紐約州
New Mexico (NM)	**New York (NY)**
北卡羅萊納州	北達科達州
North Carolina (NC)	**North Dakota (ND)**
俄亥俄州	奧克拉荷馬州
Ohio (OH)	**Oklahoma (OK)**
俄勒岡州	賓夕凡尼亞州
Oregon (OR)	**Pennsylvania (PA)**
羅得島州	南卡羅萊納州
Rhode Island (RI)	**South Carolina (SC)**
南達科達州	田納西州
South Dakota (SD)	**Tennessee (TN)**

德克薩斯州
Texas (TX)

猶他州
Utah (UT)

佛蒙特州
Vermont (VT)

維吉尼亞州
Virginia (VA)

華盛頓州
Washington (WA)

西維吉尼亞州
West Virginia (WV)

威斯康辛州
Wisconsin (WI)

懷俄明州
Wyoming (WY)

7 看看各種的動物

A What's your favorite animal?

你最喜歡什麼動物？

B —I like the <u>dog</u>.

—我喜歡<u>狗</u>。

貓
cat

兔子
rabbit

松鼠
squirrel

老鼠
mouse mice

倉鼠
hamster

馬
horse

牛
cow

羊
sheep

山羊
goat

鹿
deer

馴鹿
reindeer

豬
pig
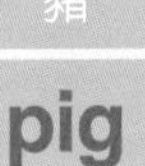

熊
bear
狼
wolf
大象
elephant
獅子
lion
犀牛
rhino
豹
leopard
熊貓
panda
長頸鹿
giraffe
河馬
hippo
麻雀
sparrow
貓頭鷹
owl
鷹
hawk
鴿子
dove
火雞
turkey

景色真美耶

景色真美耶！

What a great view!

真美啊！

How beautiful!

這真不錯。

That's neat.

真的好極了。

It's fantastic.

食物很好吃。

The food is really yummy.

我喜歡這裡的氣氛。

I like the atmosphere here.

那真大呀！

That's so huge!

這是法國最古老的美術館。

This is the oldest museum in France.

有多古老？

How old is it ?

有一千多年了。

It's over one thousand years old.

我可以拍你幾張照嗎？

Shall I take some pictures of you ?

打擾您一下，可以請您幫我們拍照嗎？

Excuse me, sir. Could you take a picture of us ?

大家，笑一個。

Smile, everyone!

開放的時間是幾點哪？

When does it open ?

禮品店在那裡？

Where is the gift shop ?

我想上洗手間。

I need to go to the bathroom.

我可以寄放我的外套嗎？

Can I check my coat?

我們在這裡休息一下吧！

Let's take a rest here.

小小專欄

☆**[How old is it?]** 中的“**old**”可以用在人或物上面。用在人身上表示「年老的」；用在物上面表示「古老的，舊的」。

☆**[Can I check my coat?]**中的“**check**”是暫存（帽子、大衣等）之意。一般在博物館等地方有“**coat check**”（衣物寄放處）可以用來暫存外套或帽子等等。

9 帶老外玩台灣

A Where are you going tomorrow?

你明天要去哪裡？

B —We're going to Yilan.

—我們要去宜蘭。

彰化 **Changhua**	嘉義 **Chiayi**
新竹 **Hsinchu**	花蓮 **Hualien**
高雄 **Kaohsiung**	基隆 **Keelung**
金門 **Kinmen**	連江縣 **Lienchiang**
苗栗 **Miaoli**	南投 **Nantou**
澎湖 **Penghu**	屏東 **Pingtung**

臺中
Taichung

臺南
Tainan

臺北
Taipei

臺北縣
Taipei County

臺東
Taitung

桃園
Taoyuan

雲林
Yunlin

A How was your trip to Lin Family Garden?

你的板橋林家花園之旅如何？

B —It was fun!

—非常的有趣！

台北木柵動物園
Taipei Mu Cha Zoo

台北101大樓
Taipei 101

總統府
The Presidential Office Building

中正紀念堂
Chiang Kai-shek Memorial Hall

台北忠烈祠
Martyrs Shrine

國立故宮博物院
the National Palace Museum

國父紀念館
Sun Yat-sen Memorial Hall

三峽清水祖師廟
Sansia Ching Shui Tsu Shih Temple

基隆市廟口小吃
Keelung Miaokou Snacks

大坑森林遊樂區
Dakeng Scenic Area

台中民俗公園
Taichung Folk Park

六合夜市
Liu-ho Night Market

愛河公園
Love River Park

墾丁國家公園
Kenting National Park

八大森林博覽樂園
Bada Forest Theme Park

太魯閣國家公園
Taroko National Park

花蓮海洋公園
Hualien Ocean Park

棲蘭森林遊樂區
Cilan Forest Recreation Area

五峰旗瀑布
Wufongci Waterfalls (Wufongci Scenic Area)

10 我要看獅子王

I'd like to see The Lion King.

我想看獅子王。

美女與野獸	貓
Beauty & the Beast	**Cats**
芝加哥	42號街
Chicago	**42nd Street**

11 買票看戲

我們購票必須排隊。
We have to wait in line to buy our tickets.

有座位嗎？
Are there any seats?

一張票多少錢？
How much is a ticket ?

有沒有優惠價？
Any concessions ?

全部售出。
Sold out.

下一個表演是在什麼時候？
What time is the next show ?

有沒有中場休息時間？

Is there an intermission ?

你們會給學生打折嗎？

Is there a student discount ?

可以給我節目表嗎？

Could I have a program please?

請給我三張票。

Three tickets, please.

兩張下星期五的票。

Two tickets for next Friday.

能否請你脫掉帽子，我看不到。

Could you please remove your hat. I cannot see.

我們可以在裡面飲食嗎？

Can we drink eat inside ?

你們有沒有較便宜的座位？

Do you have any cheaper seats ?

我要好位子的。

I want a good seat.

兩張對號票。

Two guaranteed seats, please.

表演完後，我要請她簽名。

I want to get her autograph after the show.

小小專欄

☆have to跟must都表示"必須"。"must"語氣比較強硬，含有"義務的"、"命令的"意味，通常指官方的命令，或說話人自己堅持要做某事的強烈要求；"have to"語氣比較婉轉，表示別人或周圍的環境、習慣、協約等要求某人必須做某件事情。例如：

You must not talk in class.

（上課時不應隨便說話。）

Does she have to stay at home every night？

（她每天晚上都必須待在家嗎？）

好用單字

中間的座位	center seats
交響樂團	orchestra
夾層前排	front mezzanine
夾層	mezzanine
夾層後排	rear mezzanine
包廂	balcony
非對號座位	unreserved seat
站位	standing room
白天場	matinee
晚上場	evening performance

12 哇！他的歌聲真棒

Wow ! The singer is wonderful!

哇！這歌手真棒！

電影	movie
表演	show
老匯表演	Broadway show
電影	film
音樂會	concert
歌劇	opera
諷刺短劇	skit
戲劇	play
芭蕾舞	ballet
戲劇	drama
遊行	parade
露大劇場	open-air theater

例句

太棒了！

Bravo!

太美了！

Fantastic!

再來一次！／安可！

Encore!

真是糟糕！

Awesome !

13 附近有爵士酒吧嗎

Is there a jazz pub around here ?

附近有爵士酒吧嗎？

鋼琴酒吧

piano bar

夜總會

night club

舞廳

disco

主題餐廳

theater restaurants

酒吧

bar

酒店

cabaret

小餐廳
cafe

咖啡廳
coffee shop

賭場
casino

I'll have champagne.

我要香檳。

威士忌
whisky

白蘭地
brandy

蘇格蘭威士忌
Scotch

琴酒
gin

馬丁尼
a Martini

龍舌蘭酒
tequila

不加水
it straight

加水
it with water

（啤酒）小杯
a half pint

（啤酒）大杯
one pint

今晚有現場演奏嗎？

Do you have a live performance tonight?

有服裝限制嗎？

Do you have a dress code?

我要穿什麼衣服？

How should I be dressed?

您要喝些什麼飲料嗎？

Would you like something to drink?

給我生啤酒。

Some draft beer, please.

給我波旁威士忌。

Bourbon, please.

乾杯！

Cheers!

再來一杯！

One more, please.

看棒球比賽

A seat on the first base line, please.

我要靠一壘的位子。

靠三壘的	靠內野的
on the third base line	in the infield section
靠外野的	靠本壘的
in the outfield section	behind home plate section

例句

哪一隊在比賽？

Which teams are playing?

現在打到哪一局了？

What inning is it ?

打到7局後半了。

It's the bottom of the seventh.

你最喜歡哪一隊？

What is your favorite team ?

棒球在美國是最受歡迎的。

Baseball is one of the most popular sports in America.

開始！

Play ball!

帶我去看球賽吧！

Take me out to the ball game!

你認為哪一隊會贏？

Who do you think is going to win ?

I'm a Seattle Mariners fan.

我是西雅圖水手隊的球迷。

巴爾的摩金鶯隊 **Baltimore Orioles**	波士頓紅襪隊 **Boston Red Sox**
紐約洋基隊 **New York Yankees**	坦帕灣魔鬼魚隊 **Tampa Bay Devil Rays**
多倫多藍鳥隊 **Toronto Blue Jays**	芝加哥白襪隊 **Chicago White Sox**
克里夫蘭印第安人隊 **Cleveland Indians**	底特律老虎隊 **Detroit Tigers**
堪薩斯皇家隊 **Kansas City Royals**	明尼蘇達雙城隊 **Minnesota Twins**
洛杉磯天使隊 **Los Angeles Angles of Anaheim**	奧克蘭運動家隊 **Oakland Athletics**
西雅圖水手隊 **Seattle Mariners**	德州游騎兵隊 **Texas Rangers**

好用單字

棒球賽	baseball game
投手	pitcher
捕手	catcher
打擊者	batter
教練	manager
三振	strikeout
四壞球	walk
盜壘	steal
全壘打	homerun
再見全壘打	walk off home run

15 看籃球比賽

I'd like to go to a basketball game.
我要去看籃球賽。

美式足球賽	足球賽
football game	soccer game

棒球賽	網球賽
baseball game	tennis match

高爾夫球賽	曲棍球賽
golf match	hockey game

拳擊賽	賽車
boxing match	car race

句子

你最喜歡哪個選手？
Who is your favorite player?

我是紐約洋基隊的超級球迷。
I'm a big fan of the New York Knicks.

能請你簽名嗎？
May I have your autograph?

入口在哪裡？
Where is the entrance?

販賣場在哪裡？
Where is the concession stand?

投籃！
Shoot it!

防守！
Defense!

傳（球）得好！
Nice pass!

投（球）得好！
Nice shot!

太棒了！
All right!

好用單字

傳球
pass

裁判
official

出局
foul

灌籃
slam dunk

大滿貫
grand slam

得分
score

觸地得分
touchdown

18比20
18 to 20

我的旅遊小筆記

七、生病了

1 你臉色來不太好呢

你臉色看起來不太好。
You don't look well.

你怎麼了？
What's wrong?

我想我生病了。
I think I'm sick.

我想你還是去看醫生。
I think you had better to go to see a doctor.

麻煩你打911。
Call 911, please.

醫院在哪裡？
Where's the hospital?

醫生在哪裡？
Where's the doctor?

我沒關係，我只是需要休息一下。
I'll be OK. I just need to rest.

你有維他命C嗎？
Do you have any vitamin C?

你可以做雞湯給我吃嗎？
Can you make me some chicken soup?

我需要躺下來。
I need to lie down.

你還好嗎？
Are you OK?

小小專欄

☆**[I think I'm sick]**中的“**sick**”（生病）指身體不舒服的或是生病的，通常指的是比較輕微的病；而“**ill**”（病）可能危及生命的重病，有時也指令人感到不舒服或病態。在美國除非病得很嚴重，才會到醫院去看醫生，否則如果只是個小感冒，美國人通常只是到藥房買藥。這跟我們一有小感冒，就到醫院看醫生是不一樣的喔！

2 我要看醫生

I'd like to see a medical doctor.

我要看內科醫生。

外科醫生	小兒科醫生
a surgeon	an ophthalmologist
婦科醫生	眼科醫生
a gynecologist	a pediatrician

3 我肚子痛

I have a stomachache.

我肚子痛。

頭痛

a headache

流鼻涕

a runny nose

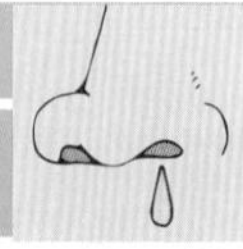

背痛

a backache

牙痛

a toothache

耳朵痛

an earache

感冒

the flu

發燒

a fever

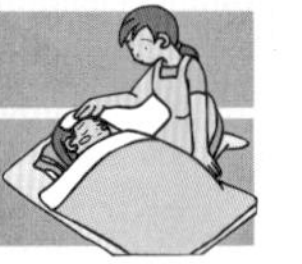

咳嗽

a cough

喉嚨痛

a sore throat

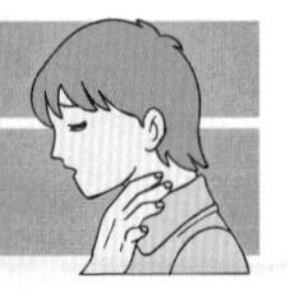

食物中毒

food poisoning

腹瀉

diarrhea

胃灼熱

heartburn

小小專欄

☆**[I have a stomachache]**是「我胃痛」的意思。一定要注意喔！這裡要用詞“**have**”，不可以用“**do**”喔！

I feel <u>weak</u>.

我覺得<u>渾身無力</u>。

渾身發冷

chilly

非常疲倦

very tired

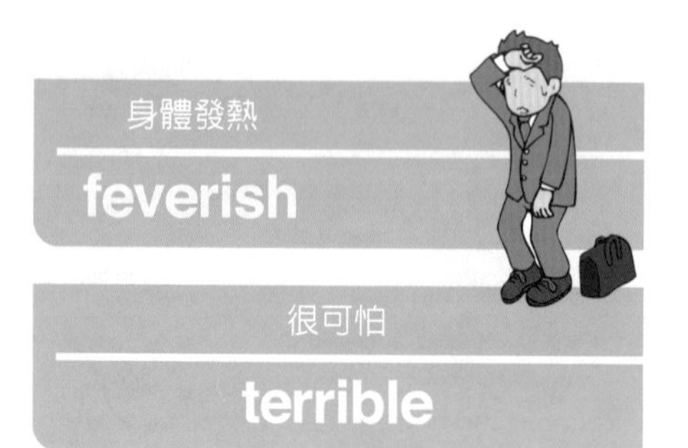

身體發熱
feverish

很可怕
terrible

想吐
sick

小小專欄

☆**[I feel weak.]**意思是「我覺得渾身無力，虛弱的」。類似的說法還有：**[I don't feel well.]**、**[I am not feeling well.]**等。

I am cold.

我在發冷。

頭暈
dizzy

昏沉沉
drowsy

對…過敏
allergic to…

便秘
constipated

句子

我感到渾身無力而且頭痛。

I feel weak and have a headache.

現在感覺好一點了。

It's a little better now.

可能這幾天我太累了。

Maybe I'm too tired these days.

希望你快點好起來。

I hope you'll get well soon.

謝謝你的關心。

Thanks for your concern.

謝謝你照顧得這麼好。

Thanks for taking such good care of me.

你有阿司匹靈嗎？

Do you have any asprin?

謝謝你的幫忙。

Thank you for helping me.

好用單字

腸胃炎

GI (gastrointestinal) **infection**

心臟病發

heart attack

高血壓

high blood pressure

哮喘

asthma

糖尿病

diabetes

骨折

a broken bone

抽筋

a sprain

My head hurts.

我頭痛。

肚子

tummy

腳

foot / feet

背

back

手腕

wrist

耳朵

ear

下背部

lower back

手臂

arm

喉嚨

throat

牙

tooth

脖子

neck

膝蓋

knee(s)

4 把嘴巴張開

你有覺得什麼地方不舒服嗎？

Do you feel any discomfort?

你會不會冷？

Aren't you cold?

我沒有胃口。

I don't feel like eating.

請躺下。

Please lie down.

這裡痛嗎？

Does it hurt ?

把嘴巴張開。

Open your mouth.

請張口說：「啊」！

Please say "Ahh".

讓我看看你的眼睛。

Let me look at your eye.

塗藥膏。

Apply the ointment.

我幫你開藥方。

I'll write you a prescription.

深呼吸。

Take a deep breath.

我們需要幫你照X光。

We need to take an X-ray.

我可以繼續旅行嗎？

Can I continue my trip?

大約一星期就好了吧！

You will get well in one week.

我需要住院嗎？

Do I need to be hospitalized?

需要。／不需要。

Yes. No.

5 一天吃三次藥

一天服用三次。

Three times daily.

說明寫在瓶上。

It's on the bottle here.

要每天服用這個三次。

Take this three times daily.

飯後服用。

Take this after meals.

不要和果汁一起服用。

Do not take it with juice.

七日用藥。

7 days of medication.

你有沒有對什麼藥物過敏嗎？

Are you allergic to any medication?

把這藥膏塗在傷口上。

Apply this ointment to the wound.

口服藥。

Oral medication.

三歲以下的兒童用藥。

For children under 3 years of age.

服用前請諮詢醫生。

Consult a doctor before using.

要喝大量的流質。

Drink plenty of fluids.

請多多休息。

Get plenty of rest.

請不要空腹吃。

Do not take this on an empty stomach.

幾天後還不見好，請打電話給我。

If you don't feel better in a few days, please give me a call.

我有旅行保險。

I am covered by travelers' insurance.

好用單字

藥局	pharmacy
感冒藥	cold medicine
退燒藥劑	an antipyretic
胃藥	medicine for the stomach
消化藥	a digestive
抗生素	antibiotics
阿司匹靈	aspirin
止痛藥	pain killer
保險套	a condom
痰	phlegm
汗	sweat
腫脹	swelling

小小專欄

☆在美國，醫師開了處方箋之後，才能到藥局付錢領藥。

6 我覺得好多了

我覺得好多了。

I feel much better.

我現在沒事了。

I'm OK now.

我好多了。

I'm better now.

我壯得像頭牛。

I'm as healthy as a horse.

我復原得不錯。

I'm doing fine.

我現在又是一條活龍。

I'm as good as new!

八、遇到麻煩

我遺失了護照

I lost my passport.

我遺失了護照。

信用卡
credit card

鑰匙
keys

照相機
camera

行李
luggage

飛機票
flight ticket

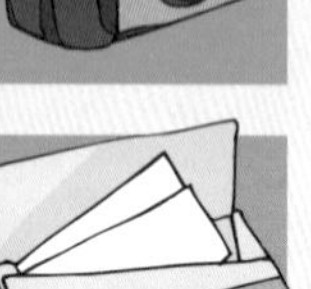

項鏈
necklace

手錶
watch

眼鏡
glasses

小小專欄

☆我們來比較**[thief, robber, burglar]**的不同：

thief:小偷。趁人不注意時，偷偷的竊取他人的財物者。

robber:強盜。以武力強行脅迫被害人交出財物者。

burglar:闖空門的小偷。趁著夜晚或屋主不在時，闖入住宅行竊的小偷。

My wallet was stolen.

我的皮夾被偷了。

飛機票	airline ticket
筆記型電腦	laptop
提款卡	ATM card
戒指	ring
手提箱	suitcase
皮包	bag
手機	Cell phone
錢	money

2 我把它忘在公車上了

I left it on the bus.

我把它忘在公車上了。

在火車上
on the train

在桌上
on the table

在計程車裡
in the taxi

在飯店裡
in the hotel

在101房裡
in room 101

在收銀台上
at the cashier

例句

不要跑！小偷！
Stop! Thief!

救命啊！我被搶了！
Help! I've just been mugged!

天啊！我該怎麼辦？
Oh, no! What shall I do?

我遇到了麻煩。
I am having some trouble.

我想有人拿去了。

I think someone took it.

請幫助我。

Would you help me, please?

我該報警嗎？

Should I call the police?

別擔心，一定就在附近。

Don't worry, it must be somewhere around here.

你可以幫忙找嗎？

Can you help me find it?

天啊！這真是棒呆了！（說反話）

Oh, man! This is just great!

我裡面有大概三 美元。

There was about 300 US dollars inside it.

小心自己的錢財。

Keep an eye on your wallet and other belongings.

小小專欄

☆我們來比較[save, help, rescue]這三個字：

help:泛指一般情況中，因為別人遇到困難請求幫助，而伸出援手的動作。

save:強調將被幫助者從危險的狀態中解救出來。

rescue:指在面臨重大危難時的有計畫、有組織的拯救行動。

附錄

常用疑問詞

一、疑問句

1 What 什麼

這是什麼？
What's this?

那是什麼？
What's that?

現在幾點？
What time is it?

你喜歡什麼？
What do you like?

你喜歡做什麼運　？
What sports do you like?

你叫什麼名字？
What is your name?

你從事什麼行業？
What do you do (for a living)?

今天是星期幾？
What day is today?

你的電話號碼是幾號？
What's your phone number?

你最喜歡什麼顏色？
What is your favorite color?

你就讀哪一間學校？
What school do you go to?

你口袋裡有什麼東西？
What is in your pocket?

你買什麼？
What did you buy?

2 Where 在哪裡

它在哪裡？
Where is it?

你住哪裡？
Where do you live?

你要去哪裡？
Where are you going?

廁所在哪裡？
Where is the bathroom?

你是從哪個國家來的？
Where are you from?

你在哪裡工作／唸書？
Where do you work/go to school?

我的夾克在哪裡？
Where is my jacket?

3 Who 誰

那個人是誰？
Who is that?

你是誰？
Who are you?

是誰？
Who is it?

這裡的主管是誰？
Who is in charge here?

誰說的？

Who says?

誰知道？

Who knows?

誰可以幫我們？

Who can help us?

4 Which 哪個／哪些

是哪個？

Which one?

你要的是哪個？

Which one do you want?

你喜歡哪一個？

Which one do you like?

哪一個是你的？

Which one is yours?

5 Why 為什麼

你為什麼會在這裡？

Why are you here?

你為什麼會做那件事？

Why did you do that?

為什麼不？
Why not?

你為什麼這麼問？
Why do you ask?

為什麼我應該這麼做？
Why should I?

6 How 如何

你好嗎？
How are you?

您好嗎？
How do you do?

我怎樣才能到那裡？
How can I get there?

天氣如何？
How is the weather?

這牛排好吃嗎？
How is the steak?

要多久才能到那裡？
How long does it take to get there?

有多少人？
How many people?

多少錢？
How much?

你為什麼會知道？

How did you know?

怎麼會(變成這樣)？

How come? (= Why?)

我該怎麼聯絡你？

How can I contact you?

＼就是這麼簡單！／

情境模擬 旅遊英語

1個句型 多個情境

每天學點 07

發行人 ● 林德勝

著者 ● 里昂

出版發行 ● 山田社文化事業有限公司
地址 臺北市大安區安和路一段112巷17號7樓
電話 02-2755-7622 / 02-2755-7628
傳真 02-2700-1887

郵政劃撥 ● 19867160號　大原文化事業有限公司
總經銷 ● 聯合發行股份有限公司
地址 新北市新店區寶橋路235巷6弄6號2樓
電話 02-2917-8022
傳真 02-2915-6275

印刷 ● 上鎰數位科技印刷有限公司
法律顧問 ● 林長振法律事務所　林長振律師
初版一刷 ● 2021年3月
書+1MP3 ● 定價 新台幣349元
ISBN ● 978-986-675-100-4
原書名 ● 《7天學會365天用的旅遊英語》

© 2021, Shan Tian She Culture Co. , Ltd.
著作權所有・翻印必究
如有破損或缺頁，請寄回本公司更換

山田社

山田社